The Dating Arrangement

—

Kerri Carpenter

HARLEQUIN® SPECIAL EDITION

Recycling programs
for this product may
not exist in your area.

ISBN-13: 978-1-335-57397-1

The Dating Arrangement

Copyright © 2019 by Kerri Carpenter

All rights reserved. Except for use in any review, the reproduction or utilization of this work in whole or in part in any form by any electronic, mechanical or other means, now known or hereafter invented, including xerography, photocopying and recording, or in any information storage or retrieval system, is forbidden without the written permission of the publisher, Harlequin Enterprises Limited, 22 Adelaide St. West, 40th Floor, Toronto, Ontario M5H 4E3, Canada.

This is a work of fiction. Names, characters, places and incidents are either the product of the author's imagination or are used fictitiously, and any resemblance to actual persons, living or dead, business establishments, events or locales is entirely coincidental.

This edition published by arrangement with Harlequin Books S.A.

For questions and comments about the quality of this book, please contact us at CustomerService@Harlequin.com.

® and ™ are trademarks of Harlequin Enterprises Limited or its corporate affiliates. Trademarks indicated with ® are registered in the United States Patent and Trademark Office, the Canadian Intellectual Property Office and in other countries.

Printed in U.S.A.

Award-winning romance author **Kerri Carpenter** writes contemporary romances that are sweet, sexy and sparkly. When she's not writing, Kerri enjoys reading, cooking, watching movies, taking Zumba classes, rooting for Pittsburgh sports teams and anything sparkly. Kerri lives in northern Virginia with her adorable (and mischievous) rescued poodle mix, Harry. Visit Kerri at her website, kerricarpenter.com, on Facebook (Facebook.com/authorkerri), Twitter and Instagram (@authorkerri), or subscribe to her newsletter.

Books by Kerri Carpenter

Harlequin Special Edition

Saved by the Blog

Falling for the Right Brother
Bidding on the Bachelor
Bayside's Most Unexpected Bride

Visit the Author Profile page
at Harlequin.com for more titles.

For John, my happy ending

Chapter One

"I'm getting married."

Jack Wright nodded his head in response. Three things had brought him to this conclusion. Number one, she was carrying a stack of bridal magazines. Number two, she was wearing a rock on her ring finger that was so large, he had to wonder if it needed its own zip code.

But the truly telling sign was the fact that she had mentioned it no less than ten times in the five minutes she'd been talking to him in The Wright Drink, his dad's bar.

My bar.

Jack silently admonished himself. He now owned the bar and had to start acting like an entrepreneur. First order of business—dealing with the bride-to-be.

"Ms. Mitchell," he began.

"Soon to be Mrs. Cross," she added brightly, clutching the magazines to her light pink dress. "But please call me Trina."

"Right. Trina. I still don't see how I can help you."

"My fiancé, Nick, and I met here a little over a year ago. Right over there, at the jukebox." She gestured in that direction, with a dreamy expression on her face.

"So you'd like to have your wedding here?"

The look of horror that flashed onto her face was so severe, you would have thought he'd suggested she get married in a maximum-security prison.

"I'd actually like to have my bachelorette party here. And Nick, my fiancé, wants to start his bachelor-party night here, as well."

While he'd attended his fair share of bachelor shindigs, he knew next to nothing about bachelorette parties. Jack pushed a hand through his dark hair and glanced around the gloomy, dank, unappealing bar. The gloomy, dank, unappealing bar that he now owned.

As if reading his mind, Trina blushed. "Although, I hope you don't mind me saying, this place seems a bit, um, different than when Nick and I met here."

What a polite way of saying it was a dump.

He sighed. "Well, my dad recently passed away."

"I'm so sorry," Trina said with true sincerity.

"The bar was left to me and it's hit a rough spot. I'm not sure that hosting a party—of any kind—is the best idea at the moment."

Trina's eyes widened. "Oh please don't say that. How about this? Why don't you think about it? I'll leave my cell number and you can give me a call." She grabbed a napkin from the bar, scribbled her number and handed it over.

Jack took the flimsy paper gingerly. He knew he needed to be frank with her.

"Trina, since you've mentioned it, I know how the bar looks now. I have to wonder why you're still so interested in having these parties here when you could go to a much nicer place."

"Because this place is special to us," she said simply.

Something about the statement clenched at Jack's heart and he had to take a deep, steadying breath. The place meant something to her. Shouldn't he feel the same way?

He couldn't reply, so he nodded his head again. A smile blossomed on Trina's face. "Okay, just think about it. If I don't hear from you in a week, I'll follow up. Plenty of other wedding plans to keep me busy in the meantime."

He'd have to take her word for it, since he was hardly any kind of wedding aficionado.

"Talk to you soon," she said before flouncing out the front door.

Since the bar wasn't open for business yet, Jack flipped the lock. Not that customers would be clambering to get in when he did open the doors for happy hour. Aside from the engaged Ms. Mitchell, soon to be Mrs. Cross, interest in The Wright Drink lay only with a handful of regulars who had been frequenting the place since Jack was a child.

Not for the first time today, his fingers twitched as he reached for the MIA pack of cigarettes he gave up six months ago.

He walked to the back of the room and glanced at the pile of bills spread across the long, wooden bar in front of him. Jack cracked his knuckles. He probably needed reading glasses. Just like his old man had worn.

His old man.

Jack still couldn't believe he was gone. While he knew his dad loved him, they hadn't been particularly close in years. No games of catch in the backyard, after dinner. After all, it was hard to do anything after dinner when you didn't usually sit down for a traditional meal. But that's what came of a dad who owned a bar. He'd spent all of his time at The Wright Drink when Jack was a kid. And the bar had thrived.

If he believed Trina's account, and he had no reason not to, the bar had taken a turn for the worse within the last year. According to several of his dad's friends, that's when his father's health had started to deteriorate. Not surprising for someone who had smoked for well over forty years. Still, no one could ever prepare for the call that their dad had passed away.

Those same friends had also informed Jack that even though his dad's health had been declining, he refused to stop working at the bar. He came in rain or snow, good health or bad. Looking around now, he could see that The Wright Drink had suffered as much as his dad.

After high school graduation, Jack had gone off to college on a baseball scholarship and played in the minors for a couple of years, until a knee injury put an end to that. He'd decided to travel. Backpacked through Europe. Spent some time in both Brazil and Iceland—talk about polar opposites. Eventually he'd settled in Vegas. He'd begun dealing at the blackjack tables at a fancy casino, as a favor to a friend. He'd actually enjoyed interacting with different people every night. He had worked hard and moved up the ranks, until he was a supervisor, overseeing the whole casino floor.

Jack began to pace; his long legs were eating up the distance from behind the bar, through the area of high-top tables and past the cluster of wall-mounted television sets. Another trait he'd inherited from his father.

Still, no amount of walking was going to get him out of this jam. His father had died of a very sudden heart attack, and he'd left the bar and his house to Jack. The Wright Drink had seen better days. It needed a cosmetic overhaul. It also needed a financial miracle. The pile of bills wasn't going to shrink itself.

In their weekly—okay, sometimes more like biweekly—phone calls, James Wright had never let on that he was in trouble. If he had…

Jack stopped pacing. He would have what? Dropped what he was doing and rushed back home to Virginia? Probably not. The painful grasp of guilt wrapped around his heart and squeezed.

His mother had died when he was a freshman in high school. Both he and his dad took her death hard. His dad retreated into himself. As the owner of a business, he'd already spent a ton of time at the bar, but after his mother's death, his dad had managed to devote even more time and attention to work. He'd stopped asking how school was going or putting in appearances at Jack's baseball games.

He'd stopped caring.

Jack and this bar were the only things his father had. Although, only one of them seemed to get any attention from the old man.

Jack tried—mostly unsuccessfully—to shake off the sullen mood. He started to make his way into the small room his dad used as an office, when someone rapped on the front door.

Jack really wanted to tell whoever it was that the bar was still closed, but he was in no position to turn away possible business. He made easy work of crossing the room and opened the door to find his father's lawyer and good friend standing there, holding a large tote bag, a small dog and a big grin.

"Jack, my boy, how's it going?"

Fred Koda had been calling almost every day. Sadly, Jack's answer to his standard greeting never changed.

"Same."

Jack eyed the dog in Fred's arms. He judged him to be about twenty, maybe twenty-five, pounds. He was a very light beige color and had lots of fur; he definitely had to be part poodle. He had a light brown nose, which his little pink tongue darted out to lick. Jack peered closer. The dog had green eyes. Very human-looking green eyes.

"I didn't know you had a dog," Jack said.

"I don't." Fred held the dog out to Jack. "But you do." Jack froze. "Excuse me?"

Fred pushed the dog into Jack's arms. The dog immediately licked Jack's chin. Fred waltzed into the bar. "This was your dad's dog."

What the what? "My father never mentioned a dog, and I haven't seen any dog-related stuff at my dad's house."

"When James had his heart attack, I went over to the house and collected all of the food, treats, toys and beds I could find. He's been living with me since that day. With you inheriting the bar and losing your dad, I didn't want to bombard you." He scratched the dog's head. "Meet your new roommate, Cosmo."

"Cosmo? What kind of name is Cosmo?" The realization hit him fast and hard. His mother didn't drink much, but when she did, she always had a cosmopolitan.

Jack followed Fred into the bar. "Listen, Fred, I appreciate you taking care of this little guy. He is a guy, right?" Jack held the dog up and looked to his nether regions. "But I can't take a dog."

Fred grinned wider. "He was left to you. You are Cosmo's new owner. But I'm going to miss our man time," he said to the dog. "Cosmo likes to snuggle and watch TV."

Swell. "That's cute and all. But seriously, I can't take this dog."

The ironic part was that Jack used to beg for hours on

end to get a dog when he was a little kid. Now here he was, shunning that boyhood dream.

Cosmo squirmed in Jack's arms until he got comfortable. Then he licked Jack right on the mouth.

"Yuck."

Fred chuckled. "He likes to give kisses." He held up the tote bag before placing it on a nearby table. "Everything you need is in here. Food, toys, files from the vet. Cosmo's a rescue."

"My dad rescued a dog?" It was so strange that he wouldn't mention something like that to Jack.

"Just about a year ago," Fred said. "I think he needed a friend."

Jack let out a long exhale, which did nothing to alleviate the hurt and guilt Fred's comment had lodged in his throat. Intuitively, Cosmo snuggled closer to Jack, wedging his little head under Jack's chin.

"Some other tips," Fred said. "Cosmo is part poodle, but I'm not sure what he's mixed with. So he doesn't shed. He's housebroken. He's also very playful, takes two long walks a day, likes squeaky toys, hates the vacuum. Oh and he's kind of a Velcro dog."

"Velcro dog? What does that mean?"

Fred actually appeared to be a little sheepish. "He's clingy."

Great. Jack sighed. "Fred, Cosmo is really cute." And he was. He would have been exactly the kind of dog he'd wanted when he was little. "But I can't take him. I don't even know if I'm staying in town."

"Why wouldn't you stay here? You have a place to live and you're the new owner of the bar."

"A bar that never gets any customers."

Fred hesitated, then waved his hand as if to dismiss the idea. "Well, I'm sure it will pick up soon."

"I'm still trying to figure out what happened here, Fred. When I was growing up, the place was packed almost every night. Now there's a handful of regulars and that's about it."

The strangest part about this was the fact that The Wright Drink was located on King Street. As one of the busiest streets in the popular Old Town area, King Street generated enough foot traffic to make attracting thirsty customers a breeze. Locals and tourists alike always seemed charmed by Old Town Alexandria, with its quaint cobblestone streets, red brick sidewalks, the history and culture, the close proximity to Washington, DC, the view of the Potomac, and the restaurants and shops.

"I'm not sure what to tell you, kid. I didn't think much of it at the time, but looking back, your dad was acting a little weird for the last year or two."

Jack shifted. "What do you mean?"

"Forgetful. Aloof. Not that he was ever Mr. Personality before."

Maybe something besides the lifelong smoking had been going on with his dad. With his health. His grandfather had had dementia. Perhaps his dad started to get the same thing.

"Do you think that's why most of the regulars haven't paid their tabs? From the receipts and records I've gone through, it seems like my dad hadn't asked them to settle for the last two years."

Fred shrugged. "Could be."

But would asking for money drive them away? Then the bar would truly be empty. Frustrated, Jack gritted his teeth. The only thing he knew about a bar was how to go to one and order a beer.

With a sigh, he said, "Maybe I'm not cut out for this, Fred. I can always try to sell it."

"Nonsense," Fred bellowed. "Your dad wanted you to have The Wright Drink. He told me many times."

"Would have been nice for him to tell me too." He hadn't meant to utter that out loud, but he couldn't take it back now. Fred paused. Finally, he put a hand on Jack's shoulder and squeezed.

"I have to get going. I'm meeting a client near Mount Vernon and I heard the Parkway is backed up."

Panic washed over Jack. "But Cosmo?" he asked helplessly.

Fred laughed as he quickly headed for the door. "You'll be fine."

"He shouldn't even be in here. There are health-code violations. Right?" Were there? He had no idea.

"James had him in here all the time. Cosmo liked to sleep behind the bar."

"Fred, wait…"

But Fred didn't wait. Jack was alone with a little dog—and with his thoughts, which was even worse.

He was in no better place than he was before. He still needed to figure out how to turn the bar around. Or sell. Despite Fred's protests, Jack was considering the idea to be a very viable option.

Ashamed of the thought, he walked to the middle of the bar. In the past, this would be the point where he stepped outside for a smoke. A little stress relief. Since that was no longer an option, Jack decided to have a much-needed tête-à-tête with Cosmo.

He placed the dog on the floor. Cosmo looked up at him with adoring eyes. "Listen, I like dogs. I do. But I'm not the most stable guy on the planet."

Cosmo shifted and then lifted his leg and peed.

Jack sighed again. Loudly. "You really going to do

that in public? In the middle of a bar where people eat and drink?"

Cosmo tilted his head, as if he were considering a reply. He just looked at Jack and walked to another corner of the bar and sat. And stared back at Jack.

"Damn it." Jack ran his hands through his hair. He swore the dog had a look on his face akin to "na-na na-na boo-boo."

Frustrated, he went to the supply closet and retrieved cleaning supplies. "Housebroken, my ass."

He cleaned up the mess and shoved the soiled paper towels into a trash bag. Then he rummaged through Cosmo's luggage and found a blanket and small bed. He stuck them under the bar, and the dog pranced over to them and made himself comfortable.

"Stay," Jack said. "I'm going to throw out this little mess."

He didn't think dogs really smiled, but this one looked to be grinning ear to ear.

"I mean it, Prince Charming. Stay."

He pushed through the back door that led to the alley behind the bar. He threw the black bag into the dumpster. Hard.

March was notorious for unpredictable weather, but today was beautiful. Mild temperature, with a nice breeze. Good day for a walk. Maybe a bit of exercise would help clear his mind. Bring a bit of clarity to his current situation.

He stepped away from the dumpster and glanced up and down the alley. He was unfamiliar with these businesses. He'd have to meander down Prince Street to familiarize himself. He did know there was a seafood restaurant, off to the right, and the door on the left led to…was it a wedding-dress shop? The windows were a little too high to see inside and protected by blinds, in any case.

Jack shook his head. So much had changed in this area

of the city since he'd returned. He was actually rather proud to see Alexandria's expansion.

Then suddenly a movement out of the corner of his eye caught his attention. He turned as a blur of white ruffles began to pour out of the window he'd just been gazing at.

What the hell?

The mass of material made a strangled sound as it continued to shimmy out of the window. A few more inches and a head of curly auburn hair topped with a veil surfaced.

He froze at the sight of a bride climbing out of the window. Either that or a life-size marshmallow had just exploded into the alley.

Yep, that door definitely led to a bridal shop.

"Gotta get out. Gotta get out," the bride chanted breathlessly.

He'd heard of runaway brides, but this was something else. He would have chuckled, but the woman suddenly slipped, leaving her and that massive dress dangling from the windowsill. He assumed her feet were under there somewhere, but it seemed like all of that fluff had swallowed them.

She let out a squeak and Jack rushed over to help. "Hang on, I got you."

Another little yelp sounded and her arms shook right before she fell... Right on top of Jack. He tried to catch her, but with all that dress, he wasn't sure what body part he had managed to grab hold of. All he knew was that he was falling to the hard ground of the alley, with a pile of lace and satin and soft woman covering him.

A friend of his caught the bouquet at a wedding once. Apparently he'd taken it a step further and caught the bride.

Chapter Two

Emerson Dewitt knew two things for sure.

First, she was lying on top of a strange man, in the dirty alley behind her mother's exclusive bridal boutique. And second, she was still wearing the ten-thousand-dollar wedding dress that had given her the urge to flee in the first place.

It was a strapless gown with a ruched bodice, and it had a fit-and-flare style, with an emphasis on the flare part. The bottom half of the dress exploded into layer upon layer of puffy white organza and tulle covered in delicate crystals and ruffled flowers. It was as close to wearing a cloud made out of cotton balls as she would probably get. Although, cotton balls didn't weigh anything. This frilly monstrosity felt like it would clock in at about eighty pounds.

And surely her savior, whoever he was, didn't appreciate having an eighty-pound dress, plus a woman, crash-land on top of him. At least the fall appeared to knock the anxiety attack right out of her—she could feel her pulse returning to normal. She couldn't believe she'd just climbed out of a window. This had to take over the number-one spot on the list of craziest things she'd ever done.

"I'm so sorry," Emerson said, shifting her weight and trying to rearrange herself and the dress. If she'd so much as knocked a crystal loose on this dress, her mother would kill her.

"'t's 'kay," the man mumbled in a deep voice. She could feel him moving under her as he attempted to push the various layers of material out of his way.

"No, it's not. Let me just…" She broke off as she tried to figure out how to get up gracefully. Only, a second later, she realized she'd left grace and all other etiquette behind the moment she'd decided to fling herself out the window.

After a few more moments of rustling about, Emerson and her Good Samaritan had freed themselves and were finally standing again. That's when she got her first look at him.

And *damn*, he was sexy. Tall and muscular, with dark, disheveled hair and dark eyes to match. Eyes that were currently giving her a suspicious once-over as he brushed dirt off his pants.

"Are you okay?" he asked.

"I am, thanks to you," she said, with her voice sounding a little breathier than she'd like. "Emerson Dewitt." She stuck a hand out to shake. He grasped it and she shivered.

"Jack Wright." He looked around the alleyway, eyeing the window to her mother's shop. "Is there somewhere I can take you? Back to the shop?" His gaze fell over her attire. "To a church?"

In spite of everything else, she laughed. "Definitely not to a church. I guess you're probably wondering why a bride would climb out a window."

He nodded gravely but there was a mischievous twinkle in his eye.

"You see, I was trying this dress on and then...well, someone must have sucked all of the air out of the room, and I was seeing black spots in front of my eyes and then..." She sighed, long and hard. "I'll take 'ways to have a panic attack' for five hundred."

Again, he nodded. "I see. Well, marriage is a big step."

She cocked her head. "Marriage?" She felt her nose crinkle. "I'm not...oh of course you would think that." She smoothed down one of the flouncy flowers on the front of the gown. "I'm not getting married." *Blew that chance last year.*

Jack remained still for a moment. Finally, his brows creased. "And you would be in a wedding dress why?"

She sighed. "Funny story."

He crossed his arms over his chest, and the motion stretched the fabric of his T-shirt, so she couldn't help but notice the rippling muscles underneath. *Yum.* She looked up—high up, because Jack Wright was very tall—to see Jack waiting patiently.

He pointed to the door of the wedding shop. "Why don't we get you inside? My dad's—that is, I own The Wright Drink. Looks like you could you use one."

"Right drink, wrong drink, I'll take either. Thanks." She glanced down and happened to notice something. Something very bad. "Ohmigod!"

"What's wrong?"

"I got dirt all over this dress. My mother is going to seriously kill me."

Jack peered at her dress. "Don't worry. I can get that out with a special mixture my dad came up with."

She arched an eyebrow in suspicion.

"You don't own a bar for as long as my dad did without having a great hangover cure and a fail-safe stain remover."

He held the door open and led Emerson through the back of the bar. He gestured for her to take a seat. She took a moment to observe the space. It was nice. The bar, a large, continuous square made of a dark wood, dominated the room. Glasses of various shapes and sizes hung from the shelving above it. And gold fixtures gave the place an old-timey feel, even if the gold needed a good polish. It reminded her of the reruns of the show *Cheers*. All it was missing was Norm and Cliff at one end of the bar.

Jack appeared in front of her, with the bar separating them. He handed her a rag. "Just dab lightly at the dirt. Should come right out."

Miraculously, it did! She was saved, for now.

"Thank you so much," she said gratefully.

"No problem."

She continued to inspect the dress and clean up any imperfections she found. Out of the corner of her eye, she saw movement and jumped out of her chair.

"What is that?"

"Huh?" Jack questioned. "Oh sorry. That's Cosmo, my dad's dog. Apparently."

Emerson clapped her hands together. "A dog!" She crouched down and the poodle-like dog pranced right over to her, with the charms on his collar jingling while he did.

"Aren't you the cutest thing? You are so handsome. Yes, you are." She lost herself in petting the dog, who rolled right over on his back. She obliged by scratching his tummy. "Do you like your belly scratched? Yes, you do." She met Jack's unamused eyes. "He is the sweetest thing."

"Don't be fooled," Jack said dryly. "He peed on the floor ten minutes ago."

"Well, maybe you should have taken him out. It wasn't your fault, cutie-pie. No, it wasn't." She took in Cosmo's adorable little face, with his brown nose. "Are his eyes… green?" she asked Jack.

"Seems like it. I've never seen a dog with eyes like that before. They're very human. I feel like he looks at me and knows things he shouldn't."

Emerson laughed. She picked up the dog and cradled him to her side, the way she would with a baby. Cosmo wrapped his legs around her and seemed quite content.

"I can't believe you're picking him up," Jack said. "Your dress."

Emerson absolutely adored dogs. Her mother had been firmly against them getting a dog, no matter how much Emerson and her sister had begged. Her dad begged too, for that matter. Of course, a dog would not have been good for her mother's antiques and perfect house.

"You better be careful." Jack wagged a finger at her. "I'm not sure if my dad's stain remover can get dog pee out of a wedding dress."

She kissed the top of Cosmo's head. "You won't go potty on me, will you? No, you won't."

"You've been warned. Now, what can I get you?" Jack asked. "Water? Hot tea? Maybe a glass of wine? I have a nice sauvignon blanc."

"A beer would be great, actually. Whatever you have on tap that's seasonal. And Cosmo needs some water."

He blinked, but quickly reached for a mug and pulled on the tab in front of him to fill up the beer. Once the frothy, amber-colored liquid was in front of her, Emerson downed half of it in a single gulp, relishing the malty taste.

A look of surprise, followed by amusement, crossed his face. "Thirsty?" He filled up a bowl with water and placed it on the floor. Emerson let Cosmo down and the dog happily trotted toward the bowl and delicately lapped at the water. Satisfied, he returned to his bed, walked in a circle and then settled into a little ball.

Emerson let out a burp. "Excuse me. My mother would kill me if she could see this." She drank the rest of the drink and held the mug up. "Maybe a water now?"

"Of course." As he grabbed a clean glass and filled it with ice and then water, he eyed her. "Want to talk about it?"

She liked his eyes. They were a dark chocolaty brown. Serious and mysterious, but there was that twinkle after all.

Emerson took a sip of the water and settled in to explain. "My mother owns Dewitt's Bridal, over on Prince Street." She gestured in that direction now. "When she gets new dresses in stock, she asks me and my sister to try them on. She likes to see them on a real person before she recommends them to a customer."

"So you were helping your mom out?"

"Basically." She broke off as she looked down at the dress with an eye roll.

"Go on," he urged, waiting for her to finish her thought.

But Emerson didn't know what to say. What could she say really? The truth? Jack might be nice, and he had provided her with some much-needed alcohol during a trying moment, but he was still a stranger. Did she dare tell him that, as soon as she'd taken one look at herself wearing the wedding dress, in the three-way mirror, the air had whooshed out of her lungs? Her heart had begun beating so fast and so hard that she could practically hear it. The room had started to spin.

She played with the straw in her glass of water.

"Emerson?" Jack asked. "What happened? You seem... upset."

She sighed. "It's stupid, really. I saw myself dressed like this and I freaked. I was being dramatic and unnecessarily emotional." She attempted a smile and shrugged, trying to make light of the situation.

The reality was the last time she'd been wearing a wedding dress, she'd been standing in the back of a church, waiting for her fiancé. But he hadn't shown. Only the note had arrived.

Jack's eyes narrowed. "Climbing out of a window is a bit drastic. But something must have made you feel that way to need to escape so badly."

"Like I said, I overreacted. I'm just not that into weddings."

Jack nodded. "You don't want to get married?"

I did. He didn't.

Not being into weddings and not being into *her* marriage were two very different things. Emerson nodded. She agreed with Jack's presumption because it seemed a lot simpler than going into the whole mess. Let him think she didn't want to get married. It's not like she'd see him again after today.

"That must be hard, since your mom owns a bridal shop."

"Understatement." She sat up straight and put on her best impression of a Southern accent. "Why, Beatrice Dewitt will have both of her daughters married faster than you can say *mint julep.*"

Behind the bar, Jack grinned. Emerson felt lucky to already be sitting down. She was a sucker for a good smile on a handsome face.

"Mama is from Spartanburg, South Carolina."

He met this information with a blank stare.

"She was a deb. You know, a debutante?"

His facial expression didn't change. She was going to have to spell this out.

"Southern women live for weddings. My mama's chosen profession only adds to her wedding-mania. Being surrounded by silk organza gowns, lacy veils and sparkly accessories on a daily basis does nothing to suppress her desire to see me married."

"But you're not engaged right now?"

"I'm not even dating anyone at the moment. But that doesn't stop Mama. My younger and incredibly perfect sister, Amelia, isn't helping matters. She got married six months ago. I'd had a bit of a reprieve while Mama was busy planning her wedding."

She clasped her hands in her lap and studied the bright coral nail polish that was chipping. Her mother had been harping on it earlier.

"So now that your sister's married, your mother is trying to get you married off, even though you're not interested."

Again, she didn't correct his assumption. Mainly because she didn't want to tell him that she had been engaged. She had done the whole song and dance.

"This year is my parents' thirtieth wedding anniversary. They're having a huge party in a month. I think she'd like me to have a date. Or a fiancé. Or a husband." Emerson threw her hands into the air. "It would complete the perfect family image. Amelia did her part."

"Is your sister as pretty as you?"

Emerson sat back and swallowed, feeling her cheeks heat up. "Um, no—I mean yes—I mean… Thank you." She bit her lip. "My sister is gorgeous. But we don't look alike. Except for the hair color." She ran a hand over her curly auburn hair until her fingers tangled with the floor-length veil.

"Amelia is tall and thin and beautiful. She looks like a model. I'm short and curvy and definitely not."

Jack took her in. His gaze swept from the top of her head, over her body, all the way down to the ground. Slowly. Surely. "I think you look just fine."

Emerson fought the urge to fidget. "Again, thank you. You've made me feel a lot better. You must be a really amazing bartender."

Jack's face fell. "I wouldn't exactly call myself a bartender."

She took in the various taps of beer, bottles of liquor stacked neatly on the far wall and rows of pristine glassware. "No?"

"I mean, I own this bar. Now. Recently, that is. My father passed away and left it to me."

The emotions on her new friend's face tugged at her heart. "I'm so sorry. About your father, I mean." She could only imagine if something happened to her mother and she had to take over the bridal shop.

Cosmo made his way to Emerson's chair. Then he let out a sound that sounded very close to a sigh. She picked him up again and placed him on her lap. He snuggled closer to Emerson.

"Poor thing." Emerson rubbed her hands up and down the dog's back, enjoying his soft fur. "I bet you miss your dad, don't you?"

"Yes."

She'd asked the question of the dog, but Jack answered. His word came out so softly, she wondered if he knew he'd said it. By the distant look on his face, she imagined not. She let it go.

"As you can see for yourself, The Wright Drink doesn't exactly have the right appeal."

Emerson took a moment to glance around the space. It needed some light—natural light, preferably. And one hell of a cleaning crew would do wonders. But all in all, she found it charming. Like an old English pub.

"I don't know," she said. "Seems like it just needs some tender loving care. A fresh coat of paint wouldn't hurt either."

"But would new paint bring customers in?"

She wasn't sure if he was really asking her, but she decided to answer anyway. "Probably not. But if you zhuzhed up the inside, spent some time on a social media campaign and planned a couple of enticing events, you could turn things around. I'm an event planner and I've done plenty of grand openings for bars and restaurants, not to mention specialized events like themed nights, New Year's Eve parties, birthday parties, you name it. You'd be surprised what attracts people."

The air hung heavily between them. They locked eyes and it took everything in her power not to squirm from the intensity pouring out of those serious eyes.

She could feel the heat returning to her face and decided to lighten things up. "I mean, there are several ways to get customers interested in a business. I just organized the food truck festival last weekend and I know there—"

"You put that together?" He whistled long and low. "That was amazing. I heard there were two dozen trucks and they maxed out on ticket sales."

She nodded. "The city wanted to focus on local businesses. Every food truck was owned by an Alexandria resident. To be honest, the publicity budget wasn't very large. But word of mouth is a powerful tool. People were excited to support the trucks."

"I got food from at least five or six places," Jack said. "There was such great diversity."

"Fifteen different ethnicities represented," she said proudly. She'd worked extra hard to make sure a variety of diverse foods and cultures were included when she'd begun organizing the festival.

"Sadly, it almost didn't happen. The organizers had wanted to do it for years, but the city kept pushing back. Said it wouldn't bring any interest. There were a lot of things we did to make sure we would pack the festival." She gestured around the bar. "Wouldn't be hard to do the same kind of thing here."

He seemed interested. "Really?"

"Off the top of my head, I would suggest a grand opening. Or a reopening, as the situation would warrant. There are several events you could begin hosting that would help garner interest."

"Like bachelorette parties?" A pained expression crossed his face.

Emerson laughed. "I was thinking more like a weekly trivia night, regular happy-hour specials and maybe even a ladies' night." She didn't even go into the social media opportunities. "You have a lot to work with here."

Jack followed her gaze. "How do you know about all of this?"

"It's part of my job."

Jack leaned back suddenly. "Looks like we both have a problem to solve."

"Trust me, it would be a lot easier to get people into this bar than it would be to get my mother off my back."

Jack rubbed a hand along his jaw. She noticed some dark stubble and could hear a scratching noise as his fingers moved over it. Was it wrong that her mouth watered at the sight?

"How about…" he trailed off.

"What?" she asked.

"Nothing—it's a crazy idea."

"Come on. We've already bonded over my frazzled nerves and your outdated bar."

"Okay then. Why don't I be your boyfriend?"

Yes, please. She coughed. "Excuse me? Why would you pretend to be my boyfriend? I mean, why would anyone do something like that? You don't even know me."

"Because," Jack said patiently, "I need your help too." He gestured to the bar around him. "I don't know if I'm going to keep this place and find someone to manage it for me, or sell it. But no matter what I do, I have to turn it around. And you'd be the perfect person to help me make that happen."

Emerson mulled over his proposal. "So you help me with my family. I help you with the bar."

"You got it."

"You're going to pretend to be my boyfriend?" She couldn't believe she was entertaining this at all. It was nuts. "That's a lot to ask of you."

"It's me being your boyfriend for one night at your parents' party. Believe me, from the looks of it, turning this place around will be the harder part."

She chewed on her lip. "O-okay. So we're going to be a pretend couple. And we'll fix up your bar."

"And no one gets hurt," he finished.

As she considered, a smile began spreading over his handsome face. If it weren't for that damn smile…

"What do you say? Do you want to make a deal?" He held out his hand and Cosmo let out a little *yip*.

She rose, and the wedding dress billowed around her. Then she clasped his offered hand. "I do."

Chapter Three

The last time Emerson had an imaginary boyfriend, she'd been in middle school. Her twelve-year-old sister had announced at Sunday dinner that she was "going with" Jeremy Swanson. So Emerson did what any self-respecting fourteen-year-old would do. She'd invented a boyfriend of her own, claiming he went to a different school and was constantly busy with sports.

That act hadn't lasted long. She'd never been any good at lying, which didn't bode well for what she was about to do with Jack.

He squeezed her hand. "Want me to go in with you?" he asked as they stood outside of her mother's bridal boutique, staring at the black-and-white-striped awning with *Dewitt's Bridal* scrawled across it in a fancy pink script. On his leash, Cosmo stood obediently next to Jack.

Emerson shook her head. "Thank you, but I think it will be better if we wait as long as possible to bring you into the fold." Easier on her, as well. "I'll spring you on them when we get closer to the anniversary party. Plus that will give us time to start work on turning the bar around."

Jack gave her a long once-over, with his face emanating doubt. It looked like he was about to ask a question. But he must have decided against it. "You're the boss," he said simply instead. "Why don't you come over tonight? I can fill you in on the situation with the bar and we can start planning."

"I'll be there. Just text me the address." She paused. "You're not a serial killer or anything, are you?"

He held his hand up in a salute. "Law-abiding citizen, I promise. But if it makes you feel better, we can meet at the bar."

She was probably being silly or overly cautious. She hoped her new pretend boyfriend wasn't a psychopath, but you just never knew these days. "The bar sounds great."

"Done. We can continue to get to know each other better tonight. If we're going to make this work, we'll need details."

Emerson cocked her head. "What do you mean?"

"If we're dating, we need to know essentials. Favorite color, movie, band, food, hobbies. I don't even know your middle name. Or if you have one."

Emerson couldn't believe she was doing this. But desperate times called for desperate measures. Pretending to be dating Jack was a tiny white lie; it wouldn't hurt anyone.

He was really great to suggest this ruse. When was the last time she'd met a decent guy like him? Definitely not any of the men her mother had tried to fix her up with. Certainly not Thad, her ex-fiancé. Thad had barely ever asked how her day had been, so he would never have stepped in to do something as gallant as this.

She eyed Jack now. Damn, he was handsome. No, she

thought. *Handsome* wasn't the right word. More like…
attractive and *kind*. She only hoped she wasn't taking
advantage of him.

She might not know him well yet, but she could tell he
wasn't the type to offer something when he didn't want
to do it. Besides, it wasn't like Jack was the only one
getting something out of this bargain. She was happy to
help Jack with his bar. And she would see to it that the
place became a success.

"Emerson? You okay?"

"Yes." His question pulled her out of her thoughts.
"Sorry. I'll be there tonight and tell you absolutely everything there is to know about me."

Apparently satisfied, Jack nodded. "Okay. Good luck."

Emerson crouched down to say goodbye to Cosmo, and
then she rose and took a step toward the shop, anxious to
get out of the overbearing wedding gown. She couldn't
imagine wearing something like this for her special day.

Before she reached for the door, she turned back, looking over her shoulder. Jack hadn't moved. He was standing on the sidewalk, watching her. He was making sure
she really was okay.

"Rose," she said spontaneously.

Jack tilted his head in question.

"My middle name is Rose."

He grinned and her knees felt weak. "See you tonight,
Emerson Rose Dewitt. And for the record, I think you
make a really beautiful bride."

Their eyes met and she had to work hard to hold back a
shiver. Finally, Jack broke the gaze and retreated down the
street, with Cosmo trotting alongside him. Emerson placed
a hand on her stomach, willing the fluttering to subside.

When she pushed through the front door and entered
the shop, she still didn't feel calm. All she could think

about was Jack. But a few seconds later, the sound of her mother's voice broke the spell.

"Emerson, finally." Her mother let out a long, exasperated gasp. "Where in the world have you been?" She rushed toward Emerson, wearing a tailored mauve pantsuit; her makeup was absolutely flawless, and every strand of hair was perfectly in place.

"I—I—I mean..."

She struggled to finish the sentence as her younger sister made a mad dash across the store. Amelia's eyes were wide and she was subtly shaking her head. "Hey, Em," she said brightly as she pushed something covertly into her hand. Emerson realized it was her cell phone. "See, Mama, I told you she was just taking a call outside."

Grateful, Emerson let out the breath she wasn't aware she'd been holding. "Right. Sorry. Business call. I didn't mean to worry you."

Her mother's narrowed gaze was almost enough to make her drop the phone and start spilling all of the details of her little alleyway adventure.

"Of course I was worried, Emerson. You're wearing a ten-thousand-dollar dress. What in the hell were you thinking stepping outside in it?"

Or flinging herself out a window. But she decided not to mention that.

"You could have gotten the hemline dirty." Beatrice Dewitt's eagle eye was already examining the dress.

"Looks fine to me," Amelia said.

Emerson took her sister in. She was wearing an elegant lace gown with cap sleeves that was straight and fitted to her flawless body. Just as she'd told Jack earlier, the two of them had the same auburn hair as their mother. But while Emerson did her best to tame her curly, shoulder-length hair, Amelia's trendy layers always seemed to float carelessly, as if someone were following her around with a wind machine.

Amelia was two years younger than Emerson, but she'd surpassed her in height before the age of ten and never looked back. Emerson topped off at a whopping five foot three on a good day, while Amelia was a stately five-nine, without heels.

Emerson had needed braces, while Amelia's teeth had been straight. During middle school, Emerson had become quite familiar with the dermatologist, while Amelia never so much as got a sweat pimple.

Amelia had twenty-twenty vision. Emerson needed glasses and contacts.

Amelia could wear anything off the rack. Emerson paid a good portion of her salary to her tailor.

Amelia had found her Prince Charming and gotten married. Emerson…

Shouldn't it have been the other way around? Didn't the law of archetypes suggest that she was supposed to be the overachiever and her younger sister was destined to be the rebel?

Emerson clutched the cell phone in her hand. The reminder that, despite all of their differences, her sister did have her back. At least that was something. And something that was a constant source of guilt.

It would be so easy to be jealous of her sister, but Amelia—her little Mia—made that next to impossible. For every success Amelia achieved, Emerson seemed to fail at something. Yet, ever since she was born, Amelia looked to her big sister with awe in her eyes, as if Emerson were the one realizing great triumphs.

And here she was, silently bitching about her curly hair and lack of height.

She mouthed *thanks* to her sister and faced their mother. "I'm sorry, Mama. Really. I just needed to take a call."

"From?" her mother asked, after her cursory examination of the wedding dress was complete.

Her palms began to sweat. "Um, just a client."

"Which client?" Her mother put her hands on her hips.

"Well, a new client, as a matter of fact."

"A new client. Way to go, Em," Amelia added. "Your event-planning business is really growing. I knew organizing that food truck festival was going to put you on the map."

She gave another grateful smile to her sister, even if Amelia didn't understand she was lying.

"Food trucks!" Her mother shook her head as her eyes rolled up to the ceiling. "Honestly, who enjoys eating from a dirty truck in the middle of the street?"

"Um, everyone?" Amelia said, with a hint of sarcasm. Emerson stifled a laugh. "Did you see how many people attended the festival? It was epic."

"Thanks, Mia," Emerson said gratefully.

"So, who is this new client?" her mother asked impatiently. Clearly they were done discussing food trucks.

"Um, well…" She almost wiped her hands on the dress until she luckily remembered that sweat stains on a ten-thousand-dollar dress probably wouldn't help her mother sell it.

"Well, what?" her mother said. "Honestly, Emerson, I can't believe you are twenty-eight years old and still stuttering."

I don't stutter. Emerson jutted her chin out. She'd been accused of stuttering since she was a little girl, when in reality she sometimes needed a second.

"My new client is a bar. They want to reinvigorate the place. The Wright Drink, over on King Street," she supplied. If she presented Jack as a client, it wouldn't seem so random when she introduced him to the family as her boyfriend, at the anniversary party.

"Don't we share the alley with that bar?" her mother asked.

Emerson blinked. "The alley? Um, I don't know. Why would I know that?"

"Are you okay?" Amelia asked, with true concern in her eyes.

Emerson's mouth was dry, her heart was beating a mile a minute and she was beginning to feel that same overwhelming feeling that caused her to launch herself out of a window earlier. She didn't know if it was because she was still wearing the dreaded wedding dress or because she hated lying to anyone, let alone her family.

"Yep, great. I'd like to get out of this getup though."

"Let me at least get a look at you two first," her mother said as her keen eye raked over her daughters, no doubt taking in every detail.

Emerson and her sister stood side by side as their mother did a circle. She stopped to dust something off the back of Emerson's dress, and Emerson prayed that she didn't notice the wrinkles from her fall, or any smudges she might've missed. If Jack hadn't been there with his club soda, not to mention being there to catch her in the first place...

She closed her eyes and remembered the feel of his strong arms around her. And the way he smiled at her from behind the bar.

I think you make a really beautiful bride.

"What's that smile about?" Amelia asked.

Emerson snapped to attention. "Uhhh..."

"Emerson, you're all flushed." Beatrice did that universal mother move of pressing her hand to the forehead. "Are you coming down with something?"

"No, just warm in this monstrosity of a dress," she covered. Emerson really hoped she didn't reek of beer or any of the gross alley smells. She took a step back just in case.

"That monstrosity of a dress is going to be a bestseller. I know it." She took another moment to collect her thoughts. "Just as I thought. Amelia, that dress is prefect for a body shape like yours. Plus it comes in white, ivory, and blush. Customers will like that. I wish I could use you in the ad campaign. Everyone would want to wear this."

Emerson couldn't stifle an eye roll.

"And Emerson…"

"I know, I know. I look like a little kid playing dress up." Emerson sighed and steeled herself for the critique.

Her mother scrutinized her for a moment before stepping forward. She pushed a curl behind Emerson's ear. "I know this dress is not your personal style, but I was going to say you look beautiful." She leaned closer and whispered, "Maybe one day you'll realize just how beautiful."

Her throat tightened.

Jack told her she'd looked beautiful, and now her mother had too. But there was one person who had never said that. It was no wonder he'd left her at the altar. Why had she even been surprised?

Stepping back, Beatrice said, "Although, now that you mention it, when you slouch like that, you do look like a nine-year-old. Stand up tall, with your shoulders back. Like your sister."

Once again, discomfort overtook her. She pulled at the dress. "I should change. Amelia, can you help me?" She didn't wait for a response. Instead she pulled her sister through the store, past the racks of tulle, beading, lace, and organza. She ignored the shelves of sparkly tiaras and the glass cases filled with elegant jewelry. She didn't stop until she was locked firmly in the dressing room with her sister.

"I really need to get out of this dress." She began pulling and tugging, trying to figure out how to get it off her.

"Okay, okay, calm down." Amelia was behind her, quickly undoing the buttons.

When she was finally freed from the cumbersome dress, Emerson let out a long sigh. She crumbled down to the chair in her strapless bra and nude panties. For good measure, she took another long inhale of breath.

"Thanks for covering for me out there, Mia," she said to her sister.

"No problem. But, Em, what in the hell happened? Where did you go? What's wrong?"

I hate weddings. I hate wedding dresses. But most of all, I hate that Thad made me hate weddings and wedding dresses.

Emerson wanted to tell her sister. But the words were stuck in her throat.

"Is this because of Thad?" Amelia asked in a quiet voice.

She really should give her sister more credit. Emerson nodded. "Kind of."

Amelia pointed at her. "I knew it. I told Mama not to have you come in today. I told her you weren't ready for this."

"You and Mama talked about me?"

"Of course," she said, as if they talked about her all of the time. "Mama disagreed. She thinks you're ready to start dating again."

Emerson saw her own horrified face reflected back at her in the three-way mirror. It wasn't that she didn't want to date. More, she knew her mother would have a list of suitors lined up, each suckier than the last.

"Maybe you should start getting out there again," Amelia offered. "I mean, your wedding—"

"Nonwedding, you mean," Emerson said.

"Sorry, Em. Your nonwedding was over a year ago. Have you been out with anyone since Thad?"

She shook her head. Amelia's eyes filled with sadness. That look was enough to have Emerson popping up and grabbing her jeans and the red blouse she'd worn when she had first arrived at the shop. She dressed quickly, threw her hair back in a ponytail and faced her sister. "I'm fine. Don't worry."

"But, Em, I, uh, get it. I do. I mean, with me and Charlie…"

She didn't let Amelia finish the thought. It was barely noon and it already felt like the longest day ever. The last thing she wanted to hear about was her sister's perfect husband and even more ideal marriage. Instead she headed toward the front of the store, ready to bid her mother farewell and get back to work. Only, her mother had other ideas.

"Oh Emerson, before you go, I wanted to tell you that my friend Suzette—you remember her, right?" She didn't wait for Emerson's answer. "Suzette is having a dinner party next week and her son will be there. He's just recently moved back from New York. He's a year older than you."

Emerson froze. "Um, I have to work that night."

Beatrice squinted. "I haven't told you what day it is." She waved her hand nonchalantly. "Doesn't matter. Also, Patty Ellington-Ross's nephew is available and I thought it would be nice for you to show him around town. After all, Patty did attend your wedding. Or she tried to."

Emerson didn't know which part of that statement pissed her off the most.

Amelia jumped in. "Mama, I actually have a guy that I think would be perfect for Em. He works with Charlie."

Emerson knew her sister was trying to help her, attempting to get their mother off her back. But she honestly couldn't tell if Amelia really did want to set her up or not.

"I don't need anyone to set me up on dates," she said.

"Of course you do." Her mother waved a hand in a flippant manner. "You haven't been on a date since Thad."

She took a deep breath. "Actually, I'm seeing someone," she shouted.

Her mother and Amelia both paused, with their eyes going wide.

"Why didn't you tell me?" Amelia asked.

At the same time, her mother said, "Who is he? What's his name?"

Now she'd really done it. She had wanted to keep Jack out of this for as long as possible. But it looked like she would have to move up the timeline. At least, she could probably keep her family away from him until the anniversary party. They should be happy enough to simply know of his existence.

"His name is Jack Wright and we haven't been seeing each other very long." She glanced at the time on her cell phone display. A whole hour had passed since she'd landed on top of Jack.

"Jack Wright," her mother rolled the name around on her tongue, the same way her father savored a good bourbon.

"Right. I didn't tell you about him because the whole thing is still so new. You know, I didn't want to jinx anything."

Her mother folded her arms across her chest.

Emerson felt obliged to elaborate. "Plus I was so ridiculously busy planning the food truck festival."

Her mother started tapping her foot. "What does this Jack Wright do?"

Not for the first time in her life, Emerson had to wonder why mothers insisted on putting *this* in front of people's names.

"He owns The Wright Drink, that bar I mentioned."

"A bar?" Her mother's eyebrows shot so high up her forehead, they might as well be across the Potomac River, in the District. "He's a bartender?"

"Yes, but he also owns the bar." Emerson could feel her anger rising. God forbid her boyfriend—or fake boyfriend—wasn't a lawyer, like her father and her perfect brother-in-law.

"Wait," Amelia added. "Didn't you just say that bar was a new client? You're going out with one of your clients?"

Thanks, sis. "That's how we met. He hired me. I know it's not the best idea, but I'll only be working on the bar for a limited time."

Silence fell over them. But the quiet was a mere reprieve, because the rapid-fire questions began almost immediately.

"How old is he? Where's his family from?" her mother asked.

"Is he hot?" Amelia asked.

"Where did he go to school?"

"What's he like?"

Jack was right. They totally needed to get to know each other. And fast.

"Um, um…"

"You need to bring him to dinner," her mother announced. "At the house. We should meet him."

"Why?" she screeched.

"Because it's customary for the family to get to know your boyfriend."

Amelia snorted. "Yeah, maybe in 1950. Mama, you are so old-fashioned."

Beatrice actually appeared shocked by the statement. "No, I'm not. I'm just a concerned mother, taking an interest in her daughter's life."

Amelia rolled her eyes dramatically. "Concerned? More like nosy."

"Fine, fine, I'll stay out of it completely." Beatrice tipped her nose into the air. "I won't ask either of you anything about your lives. I'll just stay on the sidelines, completely quiet."

"Sounds good to me," Emerson said.

Unfortunately, Amelia had a different reply. She put her arm around their mother's shoulders. "Mama, we would never want that."

Emerson shook her head. Her sister would never learn. She fell into their mother's traps every single time.

Seeming appeased, Beatrice said, "Thank you, darling." She kissed Amelia on the forehead. "Besides, *most people* think I'm quite modern, with impeccable taste. You know how in-demand this store is. We rarely have an opening for a fitting."

"Here we go again," Emerson said in a stage whispered to her sister, knowing exactly where this was going. "The reality show."

Beatrice put on an air of shock. "What? It's true. That network did want to film a reality show here. But I didn't want to expose our brides-to-be to that kind of public scrutiny."

Amelia snorted. "You may be on the cutting edge here at the store, but everywhere else in your life, you are so, so…"

"Southern," Emerson finished for her.

"And what is wrong with that? My mama knew every young man who courted me."

She saw Amelia biting her tongue at the use of *courted*.

"But the whole thing is so new," Emerson protested.

"Thursday night at the house. Let's see." Beatrice tapped her finger against her lips. "We'll have a filet and use my mama's china."

"Honestly, Mama, no one does stuff like that. We're eating dinner with some guy Em's dating, not the Queen of England."

"I think it's nice to put a little effort into dinner. Makes a guest feel special."

"I'm gonna throw up," Emerson announced.

Her mother narrowed her eyes. But after a long moment, she acquiesced. "Fine. We'll have chicken and dumplings."

"Yes!" Amelia pumped her fist into the air. Beatrice Dewitt truly did make the best chicken and dumplings in town.

"I'll even use our normal, everyday plates. Satisfied?" She arched an eyebrow in Emerson's direction.

"But, Mama, this is all unnecessary."

"However, we are definitely eating in the dining room. I will not compromise on that." Her mother wasn't listening. She was already in full-on planning mode, filling a void left after Amelia's wedding.

"Seven o'clock, Emerson. Tell this Jack to be there. Amelia, come with me." She snapped her fingers, and with a smile to Emerson, Amelia was following their mother. "Did you remember to change the bridesmaids' dresses from pink to lavender for the Theez-Porter wedding?"

Emerson turned toward the door, feeling her heart once again beating much too quickly. She'd really done it now. If it wasn't bad enough that she'd hooked up with a fake boyfriend, she'd gotten her fake boyfriend hooked up with her family.

Chapter Four

"We've been outed."

Jack was behind the bar at The Wright Drink with Oscar, the one other bartender who had been on the payroll. They both looked at Emerson, who stood across the bar from them, wearing an exasperated expression.

"Good evening to you too." He found himself amused by her yet again.

"It's not going to be good for too long, once I tell you what I stupidly did today."

"Didn't I see you not too long ago? How many things could you have done?" He exchanged a few words with Oscar, made sure he would be fine with the five whole customers who'd come in tonight, before he walked around the bar to join Emerson. She was removing her jacket. That's when his mouth went dry.

"What?" she asked, eyeing him.

"Your outfit."

She looked down, running a hand over her cherry-red shirt and fitted jeans. "What's wrong with it?" She fidgeted, and it drew his attention to the sexy boots she had on. Tall, black leather boots that almost reached her knees.

"Nothing. It's just a lot better than the last thing I saw you in." Not to mention, her face wasn't pale and she didn't have that anxious look in her eyes. Instead it had been replaced with a wild, somewhat exasperated look.

"Oh well, anything would be an improvement over that massive white monstrosity, otherwise called a wedding dress. Cosmo, my love. Hello, handsome." At her voice, Cosmo had stirred from his bed under the bar and come out to visit, tail wagging happily. She bent to pet, and lavish attention on, the dog.

Jack had meant what he'd said to her earlier. She had looked beautiful. But she was gorgeous now too. He loved the reddish-brown color of her hair and how one curl fell right over her pretty blue eyes. And he couldn't deny that he really liked her petite, yet curvy, body. Emerson Dewitt was a beauty all around.

He swallowed a lump down his overly dry throat. "Thirsty?" Because he sure as hell was.

"Sure."

"We have some iced tea, water, soda, if you're not in the mood for alcohol. Of course, we also have a fully stocked bar."

She had picked up Cosmo again and was snuggling him to her chest. "How about scotch?"

"Seriously?" he said with a laugh. Damn, the woman impressed him.

"After the day I've had, I really need one. And please go with a good one."

"You got it, boss." He gestured to Oscar, who grabbed

two glasses, even as he wore an amused expression. "How do you like it?"

"Neat."

As Oscar poured two Scotches, neat, Jack eyed her. She placed Cosmo onto the floor and scratched behind his ears. Clearly in heaven, the dog closed his eyes as his little pink tongue lolled out of his mouth.

"And I didn't forget about you. No, I didn't," she cooed. After digging in her purse, she produced a rawhide bone. "Is this okay?" she asked Jack.

Not only did Jack have no idea if it was okay for the dog, but he couldn't deny him when Cosmo was now practically doing backflips over the prospect of a treat.

"It's fine."

She made the dog sit before giving him the bone, and Jack was surprised to learn that he actually knew that command. He'd tried most of the afternoon to get the dog to do all manner of tricks. He'd gotten nothing.

He returned his attention to Emerson. "So, what's going on?"

She sighed. "The jig is up. My mother knows about you."

Jack ushered her toward one of the back corner booths. Cosmo trotted along, carrying his bone. The dog jumped up first, making himself at home between the two of them.

"I thought you weren't going to mention me for a couple of weeks?"

She took a long pull of her scotch and closed her eyes as a seductive little sound emanated from her mouth. Despite the sip of scotch he'd just taken, his throat remained dry.

"That was the plan," she said, as her eyes opened

slowly and focused on him. As if she knew where his mind had just been, she smiled slowly. Seductively.

"Anyway," she continued. "I panicked. I'm a horrible liar."

"That should be interesting, considering what we're about to do." He chuckled.

"I don't think you're grasping the severity of the situation." She pulled one leg up under her and draped her arm over the back of the booth, as the glass of scotch dangled from her fingers. It was the sexiest thing he'd ever seen.

Honestly, he'd gone through a myriad of emotions when he'd first stumbled upon her. Or, he should say, when she'd stumbled out of the window and onto him.

Jack had gone from curious to concerned, to amused. Finally, he'd had to admit that he'd also been attracted as hell. He was happy to help her out with this little ploy so that he could get some help in turn on the bar. But even if he weren't getting anything in return, he'd probably still help her. How could he say no to those light blue eyes, that pouty mouth and, okay, that sexy rack.

"Jack, are you listening to me?"

Her voice pulled him out of his musing and he hoped he hadn't been staring at her chest. "Sorry, what now?"

"I said we have to have dinner at my parents' house this Thursday. Amelia and her new husband, Charlie, will be there too."

"That's not so bad. It's just dinner."

She stared at him as if he'd just told her the Earth was flat. "This is going to be torture. You clearly have no idea what a card-carrying, mint-julep-drinking, honest-to-goodness Southern mama is like. I mean, she wanted to use her antique china for dinner."

"Is that bad?"

"It's…not right. And don't get me started on this whole

reality-show delusion she has. I mean, we showed her one episode of *Say Yes to the Dress* and she thinks she's TV-ready."

He was having a hard time keeping up with her. "What's *Say Yes to the Dress*?"

His question seemed to snap her out of her rant. "Never mind." Finally, she took a breath. "Where is your mom, by the way?"

His face fell. Even after all of this time, his heart still ached for his mom. "She died when I started high school."

"Oh Jack."

She reached over and placed her hand over his. The shock of her skin on his was immediate and electric. He'd never experienced anything like this sensation before— not with any woman he'd ever met before. Her fingers curled around his hand and squeezed. He might as well have eaten a big bowl of chicken noodle soup. His entire inside warmed.

"Thanks. It was tough, but it was a long time ago." He knocked back more scotch, anxious to change the subject. "So, I don't understand why this dinner is going to be so terrible." He nudged her leg with his and she smiled.

"We are going to be so grilled about our 'relation-ship'—" she made little quotes with her fingers "—we might as well pierce ourselves with kabob sticks and jump on the barbecue now."

He laughed. "I don't want to be just another charred kabob, so let's tackle this problem one step at a time."

She took three calming breaths, put her scotch on the coffee table and then placed her hands primly on her lap. "First, we need to get to know each other."

That was easy enough, he thought. Plus he'd like to get to know more about the intriguing Emerson Rose Dewitt. "How about a rapid-fire Q and A session? I'll go first," he said, without waiting for her to respond. "I already know your middle name. Mine is Martin, after my grandfather. What's your favorite color?"

"Pink," she said with a nod. Then she jerked forward. "No, purple. Well, it used to be pink, but I really do like purple more. My bedroom's purple. I suppose you would know that if we were really dating and you weren't just my fake boyfriend. Although, you should definitely not tell my father that you know the color of my bedroom."

"Emerson, breathe. There are no right or wrong answers here. If you don't have a favorite color, that's not a big deal. How about favorite movie?"

He waited for her to name a typical chick flick. *The Proposal*, *Love Actually*, something with Ryan Gosling in it.

"*Die Hard*," she said definitively.

He almost choked on his scotch. Instead he got up and retrieved a bowl of pretzels from the bar. She took one and he did the same.

"You?" she asked.

"*Star Wars*, any of the original trilogy. Favorite kind of food?"

"Italian definitely," she said with a mouthful of pretzel.

"Me too," he admitted. "Eggplant parm?"

"Totally," she said, and then licked her lips, drawing his attention there.

He wondered what it would be like to lean over and just take a little nibble. She would taste of scotch and sex, he was sure.

"What about women?"

He snapped to attention. "Excuse me?"

"Women?" She grinned. "You know, the sex that's opposite of yours. Girls? Girlfriends?"

Ah. "You mean did I have a lot of girlfriends?"

Her head tilted back and forth. "More like, has there been anyone special in your life. As your pretend girlfriend, that's something I should probably know."

He began tapping his foot. "There've been some women."

Emerson waited before blowing out a loud whoosh of air. "Please, stop talking. You really are a chatterbox."

Despite himself, he chuckled. "What do you want me to say?"

"I don't know. Who was your last serious girlfriend?"

"Jessica."

Again, he went silent and she waited patiently before finally saying, "Good. Now, what was the deal with Jessica?"

He was getting the idea that Emerson wouldn't let this drop, so he decided he might as well let her in.

"Jess and I dated when I was living in Vegas."

"Ohh, Vegas. Fun. What did you do there?"

"I learned to play cards in my dad's bar as a kid. All kinds of different games. But I had a real talent for poker. At one point, I was hanging out in Europe and met this guy from Vegas. He convinced me to come back to the States with him. We returned to his hometown and I entered my first official poker tournament."

"Did you win?" she asked.

"I won that first tournament and kept winning for a long time." In the meantime, he made a killing and acquired quite the impressive nest egg.

"I liked playing, but I got a little bored after a while. I had gotten to know the owners of different casinos. One of them hired me on. I started as a poker dealer and ended up moving up to this job where I analyzed the workings of the casino and the flow of employees. I tried to build shifts around the busiest times."

"Cool job."

"It was," he agreed. "That's where I met Jess. She was a blackjack dealer. A good one. Very sassy and straightforward."

"How long did you date?"

"About a year." He would have seen her longer, only...

"Why did you break up?" Emerson asked intuitively.

He shrugged. Jack really didn't like talking about breakups. He'd much rather talk about baseball, traveling, beer, the national debt. Anything.

But Emerson nailed him with an expectant stare.

"There was a period where I was working long hours. It didn't leave much time for a social life. But it was a temporary experience. I thought she understood that."

Emerson nodded once, soundly. "She didn't."

Again, he shrugged. "I found her in a compromising position with a guy who worked in guest services."

She frowned. "I'm sorry. It must have been really hard to work together after that."

It would have been. But no way would Jack stick around after that hurt. He'd really liked Jess. Found himself opening up to her in a way he hadn't with any other woman who'd been in his life. She was funny and smart. She could throw a football better than he could and she made a mean chocolate pie.

Then she betrayed him. It stung. Badly.

"I picked up and moved," he said.

"Because of the breakup?"

"Mainly. I headed to Tahoe and found work there."

Emerson cocked her head. It seemed like she wanted to say something. He was actually curious about her thoughts. But in the end, she remained quiet.

They continued going over their likes and dislikes.

Unimpressed and finished with his bone, Cosmo curled up on the booth and went to sleep.

An hour later, Jack ordered a pizza. Normally, there was a cook in the back who made the typical bar foods: nachos, chicken tenders, burgers, mozzarella sticks and the like, but he was on vacation this week. Jack was thrilled when Emerson agreed to a supreme pie with the works. He was even more impressed when he watched her take a big bite into her first slice. Most women he'd met were less voracious in their appetite. At least in front of a man. But he liked to see a woman who could eat.

While he went for a third slice, Emerson told him she liked country music, especially anything by Blake Shelton. In fact, he would venture a guess that Blake Shelton was her big celebrity crush by the way she blushed when she talked about him.

"I stayed in Virginia for college and went to William & Mary." She frowned.

"What's with the look? Didn't like college?"

"Oh no, I loved it. It's just that, well, both of my parents went to Clemson. They weren't thrilled when I picked William & Mary."

Jack sat back. He was impressed she even got into that school and couldn't imagine that her parents weren't too.

"My sister ended up going to Clemson, so that made them happy," she said softly.

"Emerson," he began, leaning forward. "You should be incredibly proud of where you went to school."

Her eyes widened. "Oh I am. It's just that…" She trailed off as she raised her hands and then let them fall into her lap. "It doesn't matter."

But clearly it did. Something about her family dynamic was off and Jack was curious to learn more.

"Anyway," she continued, "After college, I worked for

a large event-planning firm. I really love all of the details and nitty-gritty of planning an event. Eventually I started doing my own events on the side and found that I didn't need a hundred-person office behind me. Plus I had a ton of contacts. So I started my own business. I work with a lot of mom-and-pop businesses, nonprofits and other outfits that need help planning events but don't necessarily have huge checkbooks."

Jack liked the way her face lit up as she discussed her company.

Another thing to be in awe of, in his opinion. She was beautiful, smart, funny, had attended a great school and owned a business. She was a catch and he had to wonder why she wasn't taken already.

"Damn, this pizza's good." She sat back, with a satisfied smile on her face.

"Glad you like it. Tony's is the best. Wish they could serve it here in the bar."

Her eyes lit up. "Why can't they?"

"What do you mean?"

"For the reopening party. I can ask the owner of Tony's if they'd cater. That shouldn't be too hard to organize. Actually, they might even be willing to make a deal with you and deliver you a certain amount of pizzas a night to sell."

He liked the idea. A lot. "So...you could do that?"

"Totally," she said nonchalantly. "I know the owner. I brought some business his way. I planned an office holiday party last year and had them go to Tony's, where they made their own pizzas and had a party. It was really fun."

Emerson dabbed her mouth with her napkin before folding it and placing it on her empty plate. "Now that we've brought up The Wright Drink, we really should discuss the bar a little more." She gestured around the room.

"Ah, the bar..."

It wasn't that he hated the bar. He had some good memories from the place when he was growing up. His mom taking him there to visit his dad, sitting on the bar-stools and spinning around and around until he got sick, and eating more bar nuts than was probably healthy for a kid.

"Your dad left you the place."

"Surprisingly," he muttered. Her eyebrow lifted. "I didn't expect it."

"He never mentioned it? Consulted with you?"

Jack shook his head. Why hadn't he mentioned it? Or even asked if that was something Jack wanted to do. His father's lack of communication was something that had forever troubled him about their relationship—and was something he'd never be able to go back and fix. He cleared his throat. "Not a word. He also hadn't told me it had fallen on hard times."

"Well, don't worry. We're going to fix that."

Guilt built up. He knew he needed to make sure Emerson understood the full story.

"Listen, Emerson, about the bar..."

"Yes?"

"I might sell it."

Her face fell. "What? Why? That a shame. It's such a great space."

At that moment, Cosmo let out a loud snore. With his eyes firmly shut, he turned over, onto his back, exposing every part of himself to the room.

Emerson glanced at the dog and then turned her big blue eyes on him in shock. "What about Cosmo?"

Jack gulped and shook his head.

"You're not going to keep him?"

"Honestly, I don't know." He scrubbed a hand over his face. "I didn't even know about him until this morning."

He leaned forward, propping his elbows on his thighs. "My life… Well, I don't know what I want to do next. Or where I want to go. Dogs need consistency, routine."

Emerson's eyes were wide and filled with worry.

"I would make sure Cosmo had a good, stable home before I left. I'm not a monster. I'm just not sure that I want to run a bar. That I would even be very good at it."

"I bet you would," she said confidently.

"What makes you say that?"

"I'm not sure. I mean you definitely have the customer-service experience from your time working in casinos. But, more importantly, you grew up watching your dad. That was probably the best preparation."

He never thought of it that way. "I suppose so. But in any case, I want to fix it up. I'm either going to stay and need a good overhaul so I can reclaim some business and get back into the black, or I'll make it attractive enough to interest a potential buyer. It's prime real estate on King Street."

"True."

She seemed sad at this news, so Jack tried to change the subject. "Speaking of King Street and Old Town, so much has changed. There are so many new restaurants and bars and shops."

"When was the last time you were home?"

"Five years… No, more than that." Jack tried to remember. He'd been busy. But doing what? Roaming the world, working in casinos, playing poker, shirking from responsibility of any kind. "I wasn't a very good son."

Whoa. Where had that comment come from? Emerson's eyes locked on to his. Kindness emanated from them.

"Why do you say that?" she asked.

He ran a hand through his hair. "I didn't come home very often. I didn't call as much as I should have."

"I think most people feel that way about their parents."

Agitated, he stood and walked toward one of the front windows. The customers had dwindled down to two, and they were both engrossed in the basketball game on TV.

Emerson had risen, as well, and joined him near the window.

"I was off doing my own thing. Kind of selfish."

The sun had set and shadows fell over King Street. White twinkly lights were strung in all the trees that lined the street. He saw his reflection in the glass, a reflection that showed a mixture of guilt and regret.

"How can you say that?" she asked. "What's selfish about living your life? Doing your own thing? That's what you're supposed to do." She walked closer. "I wish I had done a little more of that," she said quietly.

Jack continued to stare out at the glittering lights and all of the people dashing to different shops and restaurants. "My dad used to make me Shirley Temples," he said suddenly. He hadn't known the name of his favorite drink when he'd been a kid. He'd called them the "cherry drink" because his dad always added extra cherries in his.

"I realize now how sweet those drinks are. But man, to a ten-year-old, they were the best."

He shifted his weight. "Had my first real drink here too. A beer with the old man. He'd seemed proud to give it to me. A real moment, you know? It was after we won the championship in baseball."

Without warning, a feeling so strong and so potent took over. Grief, pure and simple, filled his entire being. The air thickened around him and he placed his head against the cool glass of the window.

Jack didn't know how long he stood there. But at some point, he felt Emerson's arms wind around him. She pressed her body against his, hugging him tightly.

Her scent, which he'd already come to know, enveloped him, wrapping him in a hug that smelled like flowers and spring.

She didn't say anything, and he was grateful. He reached down and squeezed her hands, trying to convey his gratitude. Until tonight, he'd had no one to really let go with. Funny how a runaway bride with family issues could help him gain a little perspective. He wasn't alone. Not anymore. At least, not for the next month.

Thanks to Emerson.

He turned to face her. Her head tilted, and she met his gaze head-on.

There were a lot of things Jack Wright didn't know at the moment. What he would do with the bar, whether he would stay in town or once again go off seeking more adventures, or why his father left him the bar to begin with. But the one thing that he knew for damn sure was that he wanted to kiss Emerson more than anything.

His gaze dropped to her full lips, watched them part in anticipation. Heard her intake of breath. Saw her chest rise and fall as her fingers slowly curled around his hips.

He began to lean toward her, but as he did, his phone rang shrilly. He groaned, and Emerson let out a tentative laugh.

The moment was over.

"I'm sorry," he said, with his voice sounding raspy.

She shook her head and backed up. "No, I'm sorry. We shouldn't... I mean...ah, your phone is still ringing."

He frowned. "Right."

Jack begrudgingly took the call, which turned out to be from his attorney. While he talked, he noticed Emerson walking back to their booth, petting Cosmo, and then gathering her coat and purse. By the time he got Fred off the phone, Emerson was standing by the front door.

"Leaving?"

"I think I have to."

"I'm sorry, Emerson. I think we got carried away back there."

"Listen, Jack, we're already up to our eyeballs in this whole thing. It's probably not a good idea—"

But he couldn't let her finish that thought. "I liked what happened back there."

She blinked. "You did?"

"Didn't you?" he countered. She blushed, and he thought the extra color in her cheeks was adorable. He reached for her hand. "And thank you for listening. It was nice to have someone. To talk to, I mean."

His words seemed to do the trick and got rid of her nerves.

"I'm glad. Your turn to be there for me next, on Thursday night. We have one uncomfortable family dinner to look forward to."

Jack watched Emerson walk out the door and head up the street. He waited until she'd turned the corner. He'd meant what he'd said. He did appreciate her being there for him tonight. In no way had he expected to break down like that.

Of course, there was also that kiss. Or almost-kiss. That had been unexpected, as well.

As Jack walked back into the bar, he had a feeling that the uncomfortable family dinner was going to be a hell of a lot more awkward than he'd bargained for.

Chapter Five

"Are you nervous? Don't be nervous."

Jack tore his eyes away from the large two-story brick mansion to look at Emerson, who was sitting in the front seat of his truck, in a forest-green dress and those same sexy boots she'd worn the other night. Her hair was swept away from her face, drawing his attention to the long column of her neck.

"You look beautiful," he said.

"What? Oh. Well, thank you," she spluttered. The catch of words was better than the nervous chatter he'd been witnessing since he'd picked her up at her townhouse in Old Town, and drove the twenty minutes to her parents' swanky neighborhood, down the George Washington Parkway, near Mount Vernon. She folded her hands in her lap and he noticed her nails were painted a bright red. "You're not nervous?" she asked.

He covered her hands with one of his and squeezed. "Em, I'm not nervous. We're just having dinner with your family." He turned off the truck and looked back at her. "Is it okay for me to call you Em?"

She smiled. "My sister and my best friend call me Em. Maybe we should have cute nicknames for each other. What do you think, schmoopie?"

He stifled an eye roll. "You know, I'm okay with Jack."

She laughed. "You got it, cupcake." Her smile faded, and she pressed a hand to her stomach. "Why am I so anxious?"

"I'm really not sure, honey bear." He was glad to see her lips twitch at that. "We have a solid and semi-true story. You were hired to help me with some events at the bar. We quickly got together. If we get into any trouble, we fall back on the fact that we haven't known each other all that long."

"Well, that part is true enough." She glanced at the house. "Okay, let's do this."

Jack grabbed her hand as they got out of the car and walked toward the door. As soon as their fingers intertwined, he felt that thing again. That electric buzzing that seemed to surface any time he touched her. But he had no time to dwell on it, because the front door opened and a tall man with dark hair that was graying at the temples appeared. He pinned Jack with an overtly assessing stare. But then his gaze fell on Emerson, and a warm and adoring smile broke out on his otherwise serious face.

"Hi, sweetheart." His arms opened, and Emerson walked into them.

"Hi, Daddy." She leaned back and put her hands on his chest, tapping her fingers against the golf shirt that Jack knew was one of the more expensive brands. "You look nice."

"Thank you. Your mother wanted me to stay in my suit."

He rolled his eyes and Jack realized he had the same eyes—and same eye roll—as his daughter.

"I wear a suit to the office all week. Why would I want to wear one for dinner in my own home?"

"Daddy's a lawyer," Emerson explained. Then she made the introductions. "This is Jack Wright. Jack, my father, Walter Dewitt."

"Sir," he said and shook the man's hand.

"Nice to meet you, Jack. Come on in. Your mother has been fussing over everything since you told her about Jack a couple of days ago. But don't tell her I said that." He winked, and Emerson grinned.

Jack stepped into an impressive foyer, complete with a grand staircase that wound its way up both sides of the room, to the second floor. A large crystal chandelier hung from the high ceiling. He noticed a very formal living room to one side and a dining room that probably seated at least twenty on the other. While his dad's house was more about comfort, Emerson's family home appeared to be for show.

"Your house is really nice," he said.

Mr. Dewitt looked around and shrugged. "It's all Beatrice's doing. To be honest, I'd prefer a nice little cabin on a lake. Somewhere I could fish all day and relax on a rocking chair at night."

His preference surprised Jack.

"I've been married for thirty years. The best advice I can give you is to agree. The key to a happy marriage is appeasing the Mrs."

"I'll remember that," Jack said, amused.

"I'm going to find Mama. Daddy, you're in charge of Jack. Make sure he doesn't get lost," Emerson said and then disappeared around the corner.

Mr. Dewitt turned to Jack. "Do you fish, son?"

"I do. I haven't been in a while, which is a shame. I

spent some time up in Canada a couple of years ago. Did a lot of ice fishing."

Mr. Dewitt raised his brow. "No kidding. I'd like to hear more about that."

"Daddy," a woman's voice bellowed from one of the back rooms. "Bring Jack in here so I can meet him."

"Amelia, stop screaming in the house," another female voice said.

"Speaking of the Mrs.," Mr. Dewitt said with a smile. "I think it's time for your inquisition. Are you ready?"

Honestly, the grand foyer threw him off a bit. But he was here for Emerson and he was determined to remain level-headed and calm. "I feel pretty confident."

Mr. Dewitt slapped him on the back. "Good for you." He stopped walking before they could turn the same corner Emerson had rounded. "Before we go back, I just want to say that it's great to see Emerson dating again. After what happened last year, I've been worried about her."

Jack paused. What happened last year? Something fairly serious, if the lines in Mr. Dewitt's face had anything to say about it. He'd have to ask Emerson later.

"Uh, yeah." He treaded lightly.

"Nice to have that twinkle back in her eyes."

"Right. Last year was, well…"

"Exactly," Walter nodded before a shadow fell over his face. "If I ever see that little pri—"

"Walt," a female voice called.

"Coming." Walter's features returned to normal and Jack followed him into the kitchen.

"Smells amazing," Jack said. The distinctive aroma of chicken, veggies and buttery biscuits wafted from the large stovetop and stainless-steel oven.

"Thank you."

Turning, Jack found himself face-to-face with Beatrice

Dewitt. The woman was stunning. She had the same color of hair as Emerson, but hers was pulled back into some kind of twist. She wore a frilly pink-and-white apron over khaki slacks and a crisp white blouse. Despite the casual clothing, everything about her was completely together and pristine. From her manicured nails to her impeccable makeup. But most noticeable was the confidence and self-assurance in the way she carried herself. There was no denying that she was the one in charge in this house.

"For you." Jack offered the bouquet of flowers he'd brought.

"How nice," another woman with auburn hair said. "I'm Amelia, Emerson's sister." They shook hands. "Meet my husband, Charlie." She gestured to the man in the corner, who was preoccupied with his cell phone. "Babe, come meet Em's new boyfriend."

Charlie nodded toward Jack in greeting.

"Babe, get off the phone," Amelia said, with her cheeks blushing red. She turned to Jack but didn't meet his eyes. "Charlie works so hard. It's tough to get him to take a break."

"It's good to have a husband who works hard to provide for his family." Mrs. Dewitt said before she turned her trained eye on Jack. "Speaking of work…"

"Mama, give the man a second to catch his breath before we start with that."

"I simply want to get to know this man who has appeared out of nowhere, into your life. Is that so wrong? We had all known Charlie for years before he started dating Amelia. They had a proper courting."

"Mama, no one says courting in the twenty-first century," Amelia said, with a final glance at her husband, who'd retreated even farther into the shadows.

"Jack, can I get you a drink?" Mr. Dewitt asked.

"Sure, thanks."

"I'll have a beer," Emerson said.

An annoyed sound escaped Mrs. Dewitt. "We don't have any beer. Walt, get her the same wine Amelia is drinking."

"I don't want—"

"How about a tour?" Jack said suddenly, cutting Emerson off. Emerson shot him a grateful smile.

"Babe," Amelia said. "Babe," she repeated louder.

"Leave him," Emerson said and grabbed her sister's hand. "We don't need Charlie to show Jack around. Come on, everyone. The tour leaves from the kitchen. Keep your hands and feet inside the train. No photography please."

"Unless you're from *Southern Living*," Amelia whispered, and Emerson laughed.

As Emerson and her sister gave Jack a tour of the sprawling house, he came to a few conclusions. The first was that he wouldn't be surprised if he did see this house on the pages of *Southern Living*. Each room was practically photo-shoot ready. Pillows were fluffed, tables were polished and vases were overflowing with flowers.

The second thing he noticed about the Dewitt home was that it was clear Amelia had grown up here. He noticed pictures, trophies and other memorabilia. What he did not see was the same attention for Emerson.

They walked into a family room, toward the back of the house. Despite the size of the place, Jack had been feeling somewhat claustrophobic. This was the first room that actually made him feel welcomed. There were also more personal items here.

He stepped up to a large shelf that held trinkets and framed pictures. Jack took in a photo with a little redhead wearing a tiara and holding a huge bouquet of roses. He chuckled. "Who's this? You?" he asked Emerson.

"No, that's me," Amelia said.

"Amelia used to do pageants." Emerson peered at the photo closer. "She was about five in that one."

"Did you do pageants too?" he asked, putting the frame down. "Were you Little Miss Alexandria?"

Amelia let out a very unladylike snort.

"Thanks for that," Emerson said, elbowing her sister. "I tried. And by 'I tried,' I mean Mama had me entered in pageants before I could even eat solid food. But it became clear pretty fast that runways and posing wasn't really my thing."

"How come?"

"Let's just say I wasn't quite as graceful as my sister."

Amelia put an arm around her sister. "She fell off a stage, right onto the judges' table. Mama was horrified."

"Thank God she had a second daughter."

The two sisters were laughing, but Jack sensed something sad underneath the jokes. He eyed another photo of a cheerleader waving pompoms over her head. "Amelia again?" he asked.

"Yep, I cheered all through middle and high school."

Jack quirked an eyebrow at Emerson.

"Nope," she said. "I tried out a couple of times. But I never made the squad." She smiled but it didn't reach her eyes. After turning back to the shelf, she tapped another frame. "And this is Amelia being crowned homecoming queen."

Jack thought he was getting the lay of the land. "Amelia, what do you do now?"

"I work in Mama's store."

Aha. So Amelia, the pageant-winning, cheerleading homecoming queen, worked with her mother, while Emerson, the non-poised, pom-pom-less black sheep, had started her own business. Interesting.

Jack grabbed another frame and studied it. He couldn't contain the smile. Emerson's perfume alerted him to her nearness before he realized she was peering around his shoulder.

"Ugh, don't look at that." She snatched the photo away. "I look so ugly in that one."

Amelia reached for the picture. "No, you don't. You're so hard on yourself, Em." She returned the photo and took another. "This is my favorite picture of Em." She thrust it at Jack.

Jack saw the two sisters. Emerson was wearing a cap and gown, and Amelia had on a flowered dress. Emerson was sticking her tongue out, while Amelia was making a funny face at the camera.

"Your college graduation was so much fun. Remember the party?"

Emerson giggled. "After we dropped off Mama and Daddy at the hotel and claimed we were going to bed."

They both made a weird noise at the exact same time and then did a little dance, clearly reminiscing about some shared memory.

Jack could tell they really loved each other. Beatrice and Walter Dewitt were incredibly lucky their two daughters got along. Jealousy could have easily pervaded their relationship.

"Jack. Girls. Dinner is ready," Mr. Dewitt said from the doorway.

Jack followed everyone into the formal dining room. His mouth watered at the sight of chicken and dumplings, although he had to admit he couldn't remember the last time he'd eaten in a formal dining room, with candles and flowers.

"Jack, want to help me pick some music?" Mr. Dewitt asked.

Jack walked over to the side of the room, where he was surprised to find a record player and a shelf filled with vinyl records. He perused the collection. "Now, this is impressive."

He clapped Jack on the back jovially. "Some people think my selection is old."

"Nothing wrong with oldies," Emerson said before she and her sister started doing a little dance as Amelia sang "Here Comes the Sun."

"No respect for the best music of all time," Mr. Dewitt said. But he was smiling as he watched his girls joking. "I'm telling you, this was music. I can't even categorize what you people listen to now."

Jack and Mr. Dewitt went through the records, while Mrs. Dewitt and her daughters brought the food in. Jack loved seeing the album covers from the Beatles, The Mamas & the Papas, and other groups from the sixties and seventies. They ended up choosing an album of Chicago's music.

"Amelia, where's Charlie?" Mrs. Dewitt asked.

"Oh he said he needed to make one more call. We should go ahead and start though."

Mr. Dewitt said grace and they all dug in. The food was delicious, the wine was amazing and the conversation flowed. Charlie eventually made his way in, but even Jack could tell he wasn't giving anyone his full attention. Charming guy, he thought.

"We're sorry to hear about your father's passing, Jack," Mrs. Dewitt offered. "Emerson explained that it happened recently."

"Yes, and quite suddenly. Thank you for the condolences."

"I understand he left you The Wright Drink. I used to pop in there," Mr. Dewitt added.

"When?" Mrs. Dewitt asked, with eyes narrowed.

"Quite frequently actually. I didn't know your father well, but he was always kind and a great bartender. The bar is only a couple of blocks from my office. It's over on Washington."

Mrs. Dewitt leaned forward. "And what were you doing before you became the owner of a bar?" She said *bar* the way some people might say *serial killer*.

"A lot of different things actually. I traveled quite a bit after college."

Mrs. Dewitt eyed him over the rim of her wineglass, and Jack had the distinct impression that she knew exactly what he'd been doing. Nothing. Floundering as he traveled the world, trying to find himself. Staying away from Alexandria and not helping his father.

Of course, he wouldn't say any of that. "The last place I lived was Tahoe. I was working for one of the casinos. I was a floor manager."

Apparently this career didn't please Mrs. Dewitt. She remained still.

But Amelia popped up. "I adore Tahoe. What a fantastic place."

"You've been?" Jack asked.

She nodded. "A couple of times actually. I've competed in several pageants on the West Coast."

Finally, Mrs. Dewitt smiled. "Amelia was a top competitor on the beauty-pageant circuit. She always placed."

Jack didn't really know what that meant. "And Emerson? What was your thing?"

"Emerson didn't really have a thing," Mrs. Dewitt said.

"I played soccer," Emerson said quietly. "And I was a good student."

Ignoring her daughter, Mrs. Dewitt continued. "Amelia seemed to get all of the performing talent in the family. She probably could have kept competing too. But she opted for college instead. Of course, you enjoyed your time with your sorority sisters, didn't you, sweetie?"

Amelia shifted in her chair. "Um, actually…"

"Emerson didn't get into a sorority."

"That's probably because I didn't even pledge one," Emerson said quietly. "It wasn't my thing."

"It's a shame, that's what it is," Mrs. Dewitt said. "You could have gotten into any sorority you pledged. You would have made a wonderful Kappa."

Emerson rolled her eyes. "I didn't want to be a Kappa. Or a member of any other sorority," she added. "Just like I didn't want to compete in beauty pageants."

"You could have done really well in pageants." Mrs. Dewitt took a delicate sip of her wine.

Emerson, her sister and Mr. Dewitt all exchanged glances before breaking out into laughter.

Mrs. Dewitt tilted her head, and her perfectly straight nose pointed in the air. "So you fell off the stage one time. I would have gotten you a coach. You could have been amazing. With all that curly hair, you would have really stuck out."

Emerson scoffed. "I think I would have stuck out because I was about half a foot shorter than most of the other contestants."

Mrs. Dewitt considered. "True. Amelia did get all of the height between the two of you."

This conversation felt very weighted in Amelia's direction. Jack felt for Emerson. He wanted to squeeze her hand or, hell, wrap her in a massive hug. But she was seated across the table from him. He'd have to try to save her another way.

"Emerson's event-planning business seems to have really taken off," he said. He noticed that Emerson had her eyes trained on her nearly empty plate. "I can't believe she put that food truck festival together single-handedly. People are still raving about it. And it's brought a lot of business to the area." She gave him a grateful look and he winked at her.

Mrs. Dewitt waved a hand. "Yes, yes. But why people want to eat food from a truck is beyond me. I prefer a nice crisp salad."

"There are food trucks that serve salads, Mama," Amelia said.

"Hmm."

"Well, I'm still impressed that Em did the whole festival," Jack said.

Beatrice picked up her wineglass and twirled it in her hand. "Emerson with her business and Amelia married and getting ready to start a family."

Jack practically heard bells and angelic chimes when she said the word *married*. In his opinion, starting a business was a hell of a lot harder than getting married. And continuing to run it alone was even ballsier.

Mr. Dewitt raised his glass. "We have two successful daughters."

Charlie, who finally tore his eyes away from his phone, although it was positioned right next to his plate, decided to weigh in on the conversation. "Totally. And personally, it's better that you and Thad didn't go through with the wedding, Emerson. He used to tell me that he didn't like the idea of you working so much and that after you were married, he would get you to slow down. Who would have managed the food truck festival then?"

It felt as if all of the energy had been zapped from the room. Everyone seemed to be looking anywhere but at each other.

Jack froze. He obviously didn't know the particulars,

but something had him holding his breath. Emerson had almost gotten married? Why didn't he know that? Because the other night he'd been so busy lamenting his relationship with Jess that he'd never asked Emerson about her past relationships.

To his credit, Charlie didn't appear to realize he'd shoved his large designer-clad foot in his mouth. He shoveled chicken and dumplings into his mouth right before he added, "I never really liked Thad. Jack seems way cooler."

Jack snuck a glance at Emerson. Her face was beet-red and her eyes held a shine, as if she were about to…cry?

Emerson's mother coughed. "Everyone stumbles from time to time. What happened last year is over," she said with a head nod.

What in the hell happened last year? Jack wanted to scream the question out. But he didn't have a chance, because Emerson had scooted her chair back, excused herself and quickly rushed from the room.

Oblivious to the awkward moment he'd created, Charlie stood as well. "I need to make a call. Be right back, babe."

Amelia let out a sigh.

Mrs. Dewitt put her wineglass down with a frown. "Maybe I should go talk to Emerson. I don't know why she gets so worked up."

Maybe because you devalue her at every turn. Maybe because she's constantly compared to her sister. Maybe because something painful happened last year and it was just thrown in her face.

But Jack kept that all to himself. Instead he rose, mumbled his excuses and left the room to find his fake girlfriend.

Emerson made her way through the house, to the patio door, and kept walking until she'd wound through her

mother's extensive garden and found herself sitting in
the gazebo, at the back of the property.

The air was cold and crisp. Even as it felt good on her
overheated skin, she shivered, and wished she'd brought
her jacket with her. Next thing she knew, someone was
draping it over her shoulders.

She looked up to find Jack studying her.

"Hi," he said.

"Hi."

Emerson couldn't say more. She was too embarrassed
to really go into anything. Her mother had massively hu-
miliated her in front of Jack. Although, Emerson didn't
know what was worse—that her mother had brought up
her biggest failure to date or the mere fact that she'd had
such a failure to begin with.

Added to that was the fact that her perfect sister hadn't
been left at the church on her wedding day.

How could she compete with Amelia? She couldn't.

Jack sat down next to her on the built-in bench.

"Thanks for the coat," she said.

"No problem, schmoopie." He stretched his long legs
out in front of them. "And see, you were worried that your
family would know we were lying."

"Silly me."

"Are your family dinners always like that? Because,
let me tell you, I'd have gotten myself adopted into a new
family by now."

She tried to smile but suddenly felt too tired to put in
the effort. "I should be used to it by now. It's just that my
sister is so amazing."

"She's okay," Jack said. "You're more interesting."

"You don't have to say that."

"I wouldn't say it if it weren't true. Your sister basically spent her youth parading around stages and at foot-

ball games. Now she works in your mom's bridal shop. And she has a husband who probably wouldn't notice if she sprouted three heads and flew away to Mars."

That got her attention. Emerson faced him. "What are you talking about?"

"Your brother-in-law is kind of a…"

"Perfect husband?" Emerson supplied. "Hard worker, good provider, top attorney?"

"I was going to say douche but sure, we can go with your words."

Emerson's mouth fell open.

"Come on, Em. We've been here for a couple of hours and he's been on his phone for most of that time. He's ignored his wife and been rude to his in-laws. My dad sure as hell would never have let him get away with that."

Charlie had been in her life for years now. Ever since he started working at her dad's firm, while he was still in law school. If she was being honest, she didn't really know much about her sister's husband, despite the fact that he'd been around for years. Jack was right. Charlie *was* a bit absent.

"I guess you're right," she said. "I'm still sorry you had to witness all of that in there." She pointed toward the house.

He scooted closer. "Well, the food was good. The drinks were great. The music was fantastic. Your parents' house is beautiful and fancy. I could have done without the post-dinner let's-make-Emerson-feel-bad conversation."

She let out a long, drawn-out sigh. "I hate disappointing people."

Jack grabbed her shoulders and turned her to face him. "What in the hell are you talking about? You haven't disappointed anyone. How could you? By not being in beauty pageants, cheerleading or a sorority? Come on."

"All of those things are important to my mother. And I was never any good. To top it off, last year…well, I probably achieved my biggest failure yet."

Jack dropped his hands. "I don't know what happened last year, but I can only tell you that I think you're amazing." He pushed an errant curl back behind her ear, and his fingers lingered for a few seconds. Emerson's breath caught in her throat.

She wondered if she should just tell him the truth. All of it. Every dirty detail about what had gone down last year. Surely Jack was curious, after everything that had been said tonight. Only, she really didn't want to talk about it. In fact, she wished she could blink her eyes and erase it from her personal history.

"You know, failing at stuff would be a lot easier if I were an only child. But there's Amelia. She's beautiful."

"You're beautiful."

Emerson shook her head. "She's smart."

Jack gently cupped her cheek with his hand. "You're smart. Really smart." His thumb traced a slow circle along her skin, eliciting shivers.

He'd moved even closer. Or maybe she'd done that. Emerson didn't know. All she could tell at the moment was that she was practically in Jack's arms and she hadn't felt this good in ages.

"Amelia doesn't mess up," she whispered.

"That's not very interesting." He lowered his head. "She's…"

"Not you," he finished. With that, Jack covered her mouth with his.

Emerson let out a surprised gasp but couldn't stop her arms from snaking around his neck. His lips were soft, but urgent, as they moved over hers. He ran his hands through her hair and emitted a satisfied sound.

She could taste the wine on his lips and smell the cologne he'd put on. And those talented lips continued to delight her. He now ran his hands up and down her back, pulling her even closer. She felt safe and warm cocooned in his arms.

While their kiss may have begun gently, even sweetly, it was beginning to pick up steam. Her mouth opened for him and she felt his tongue sweep in to tangle with hers. Her breathing was labored, and her heart rate was sky-high.

"Oops, sorry, guys."

Emerson jumped back, and Jack's eyes darted around at the sound of Amelia's voice.

"I was just making sure you were okay, but I can obviously see that you are. Sorry again."

Emerson snuck a glance at Jack. He seemed as dazed as she was. She stood, with her chest rising and falling rapidly from the exertion of the kiss.

"Um, that's okay," she told her sister, even though the interruption was pretty much as far from okay as it could get. "We should probably get back inside."

Jack looked like going inside was the worst idea ever and she almost laughed out loud. Reluctantly, he followed her as Amelia led them both through the garden.

Maybe her sister's interruption came at the perfect time. Maybe she shouldn't be kissing Jack at all. After all, their whole relationship was fake.

Only, that kiss hadn't felt fake.

Out of all of the things that had gone wrong tonight, Jack's kiss was the only thing that had felt right.

Chapter Six

Emerson had woken up with a headache the size of the National Mall.

It didn't help matters that she had berated herself from the second she got out of bed. Even while showering and getting ready for the day, she couldn't stop being annoyed with herself. The short walk from her townhouse to the local coffee shop had allowed her more time to criticize. Even during her morning meeting with a potential client, she had lost focus and begun mentally scolding herself.

She'd done a lot of irresponsible things throughout her life, but kissing Jack was possibly the dumbest, most irresponsible one of them all.

Well, maybe the second most irresponsible move, after climbing out the window of her mom's shop in that wedding dress.

Even now, as she sat at the desk in her office, all she could do was try to figure out what in the heck she'd been thinking. The two of them were already up to their eye-balls in lies and a complicated relationship. Not to mention the fact that Jack was a short-timer.

She'd certainly been disappointed the other night, when he'd revealed that he might not keep the bar. Even though he said he hadn't completely made up his mind about staying in Alexandria, she had a strong feeling that he would be out of there as soon as he could.

The worst part was that, while she rationally knew that kissing him had been beyond stupid, she couldn't stop remembering how it had felt. He was a damn good kisser. Not that she had oodles of experience, but from what she did know, he was head and shoulders above the rest.

"Hello!"

At the exasperated voice of her best friend, Grace, bellowing over the phone, Emerson finally pulled herself out of her funk.

"Sorry, Grace."

"What's with you today? Are you having second thoughts about not writing up a formal contract? Because this wedding is a really, really big deal, and I know the guest list is reaching seven hundred, and I could really use your help, and I really love you."

Emerson couldn't help but laugh. "How many *really*s did you just use?"

"Too many?"

Emerson could just see her friend now. She would be sitting behind her desk, with her long beautiful black hair perfectly styled. No doubt she was crossing her fingers, waiting on Emerson's reply.

She and Grace had met right out of college, when they had both just been starting out at a large event-planning company in DC. The work had been grueling. They'd worked long days, getting coffee for higher-ups, doing boring tasks no one else wanted to do and bonding beyond belief. They'd become roommates and the closest of friends.

Emerson had lasted two years before she moved on to work for a smaller event firm; Grace had made it a few months longer. But their friendship had endured through all of these years. They'd lived together, until last year, when Emerson had moved into the townhouse she was *supposed* to share with her soon-to-be-husband.

After the nonwedding debacle, Thad gave her his share of the property. He'd acted like he was doing it as a goodwill gesture. Emerson just remembered how terrified she'd been. She couldn't afford the mortgage on a three-story townhouse in the heart of Old Town. Not by herself. Especially after just starting a new business. But her pride hadn't allowed her to admit that to Thad.

After a couple of terrifying weeks of thinking she was going to have to return to working for other people, she'd been struck with inspiration. To her delight, Thad had never moved in, but Grace had. She was living with Emerson and paying rent.

They'd converted the bottom floor, turning it into offices. Emerson had set up shop on one side of the first floor, and Grace, who had also started her own business as a wedding planner, was right across the hall. The two of them lived on the upper two levels and could boast the best commute in the city.

Emerson glanced around her office space now. She absolutely adored it. She'd painted the walls a neutral and calming gray tone. The floors were a light wood, large windows faced the street and the walls were trimmed with gorgeous crown molding that had probably been added in the 1920s. She'd added touches of color with a turquoise area rug and matching throw pillows on the chairs and the small couch. She'd installed a glamorous miniature chandelier and had a dozen mirrors in various shapes and sizes on one wall, to pick up the sparkling crystals. The gray-and-turquoise curtains tied everything together. The space was clean but fun. The perfect area to talk about events and parties.

"I'm sorry, Gracie. I have a lot on my mind today."

"Say no more."

With that, the line went dead. Emerson laughed, because she knew exactly what her friend was up to. In fact, she could have timed her.

Ten minutes later, right on the dot, Grace waltzed through the front door of Emerson's office, with two coffees in hand. She handed one to Emerson, then sat in the chair reserved for clients, crossing her graceful legs and smoothing down her hair.

Grace Harris was stunning. She had thick black hair that fell well below her shoulders. Her skin was flawless, which made her gorgeous green eyes stand out. She was tall, with legs for days. She was wearing a lilac-colored wrap dress, with nude heels, and carried a plum-colored tote.

After she handed over Emerson's preferred coffee drink, she produced a white paper bag from their favorite local bakery, out of her Kate Spade tote. "Chocolate croissant?"

"God, yes," Emerson said around a happy sigh.

"I really should hate you, you know." Emerson took a large bite of the croissant. "This is so great."

Grace simply arched a dark eyebrow in response.

"I mean, look at you. You resemble a damn Disney princess. Why are you so perfect at this hour of the morning?"

Finally, Grace sat forward. "As much as I love you

gushing about me, I'm going to go out on a limb and guess that something is bothering you."

Emerson fell back against the chair and sighed. "You're perceptive too."

Grace began tapping her fabulous shoes in a quick staccato against the hardwood floors.

"I kinda did something stupid."

The toe tapping halted, and Grace waited patiently. Emerson told her about the wedding-dress freak-out.

"Wait a minute." Grace flung a finger into the air. "You climbed out of a window and into a dirty alley, wearing the new Pnina Tornai gown?"

"Guilty."

She reached inside her tote, pulled out her iPad and made a quick note. "I have got to get over to your mom's shop to see that dress. I have a bride who is going to do backflips for it."

"It wasn't very comfy."

"Of course it wasn't comfy. It costs ten thousand dollars."

Idly, Emerson wondered what a person would have to shell out for comfort. Fifteen thousand? Twenty?

"What happened next?" Grace asked.

Emerson told her everything as the two of them drank their coffee and ate their chocolate croissants. She filled her best friend in on meeting Jack—well, falling on top of Jack—the bar, the arrangement they made and the dinner at her parents' house. She told her every detail, up until their kiss.

"I can't believe your brother-in-law brought up Thad in front of Jack. Actually, I can believe it. I love your family, but man, Charlie is out of touch." Grace threw away their trash and returned to her seat. "That must have been awful though."

"It was. But then…"

Grace tilted her head. "Then what?"

"Then Jack found me outside, in the garden."

Grace leaned forward, and her eyes were sparkling. "Ohmigod."

"Grace, stop it."

Emerson loved her BFF but she knew that look. Grace was in love with love. She watched romantic comedies, read romance novels nightly and put up Valentine's Day decorations on the same day that she took down her Christmas tree. She was the most romance-loving person on the planet, and any hint of love in the air set her over the edge.

"I can just see it now." Grace's face softened, and she got that dreamy expression that Emerson knew all too well.

"And we've lost her, ladies and gentlemen," Emerson said.

"You were upset. You ran off into the garden and the cool, crisp night. You ended up at the gazebo." She quickly looked up. "The twinkly lights came on."

"There were no twinkly lights."

"There you were, under the glow of the moonlight, which cast a halo-like aura around your fabulous red hair."

"My hair is auburn."

"And then Jack came out and swept you into his arms and kissed you as the orchestra music swelled."

"I think there was a dog barking in the background."

"He did kiss you, didn't he? Tell me you guys kissed."

Emerson crinkled her nose. She wanted to hold out. She desperately wanted to keep the make-out session to herself. If, for no other reason, that she was still trying to justify her actions. But how could she resist Grace's hopeful face. She nodded.

Grace let out a squeal that only that dog from the night before could hear.

"This. Is. So. Exciting." Grace punctuated each word as she did a little dance in her chair.

"Exciting? Are you nuts?"

"You have a boyfriend!"

Emerson shook her head. "I have a pretend boyfriend, and I'm lying to my entire family about him."

"Maybe he's your soul mate. Maybe you're going to marry him. Maybe I'll get to plan your wedding." She finished with another squeal.

"I'm not thinking about marrying him, Grace. Or anyone," she quickly added. "I'm afraid I might be thinking about sleeping with him though. Ugh." She flung her head onto the desk.

"What's wrong with sleeping with him? You're both adults. Is he attractive?"

"Oh good Lord, yes. That's the problem."

"That doesn't sound like a problem to me."

"Every time I'm around him, I just want to…to…jump his bones," she finally finished.

"What's stopping you?" Grace wondered.

I'm scared. She should have been married for a year already. But Thad hadn't only called it off; he'd broken up with her in the most humiliating and public way.

But if Emerson was being honest with herself, she'd had a feeling that something was off. In her profession, growing up helping her mother out at the wedding shop, and even with assisting Grace, she was around brides and weddings constantly. A bride could be stressed out beyond belief, but they still managed to have a certain glow. There was an excitement, an anticipation, that came with being engaged.

Emerson had never felt that. Sure, she'd been happy

when Thad had proposed. They'd been dating for two years. He had given her his mother's cushion-cut diamond ring. They'd taken professional engagement photos. She'd registered for a china pattern that she didn't really like but her mother had insisted was amazing.

Between her business, planning the wedding and buying the townhouse, she hadn't had time to really ask herself if she was in love with him. Well…she hadn't allowed herself that time. If she had, Emerson would have had to admit the truth.

"I don't know if I'm ready to be with a man again," she said to Grace. "In that way or any other way. It's too soon."

Grace reached across the desk and squeezed her hand. "It's been a year, Em. It's time to get back out there."

Suddenly uncomfortable, Emerson started fidgeting in her seat. "I'm happy, you know."

"I know."

"I love my job. I have a great house. Fabulous friends."

Grace smiled. "I know," she repeated. "But did you ever think that you could have more?"

More sounded scary. She'd had more. She'd lost it.

Emerson didn't like the serious feeling that was permeating the air, so she shook her hands in front of them as if she was wiping away the mood. "It doesn't matter anyway, because Jack is in the middle of some major life changes. His dad just passed away. He's been given this bar. And he inherited a dog."

"Ooohh, a dog! Men with dogs are so hot."

"He's really cute too. The dog, I mean. His name is Cosmo and he is just precious." She took a long breath. "But he doesn't really want the bar. He doesn't even know if he's going to stay in the area."

"What do you mean?" Grace looked shocked. "He's not going to live here?"

"Maybe not."

Grace appeared to be deep in thought. "You like him."

"I just met him."

"You like him. I can tell. But if he's going to be leaving soon, you really need to protect yourself. I don't want to see you get hurt again. You've already committed to this lie with him. But try to keep your wits about you. You don't want to get in too much further at this point."

They began talking about the wedding Grace needed help with. Emerson was happy for the topic change.

Still, her friend's words were echoing throughout her mind. She didn't want to get hurt again either. Yet she had the feeling she was already in way too far with Jack.

Jack didn't consider himself an indecisive person. Nor did he scare easily. Yet he'd picked his phone up and considered calling Emerson, before returning it to his pocket, about a hundred times already.

Once again, he unlocked the screen and studied her name. He hadn't heard from her since Thursday night, when they'd had dinner with her parents.

Since you kissed her.

He shoved a hand through his hair. "Christ," he said into the silence of the empty bar. It was only Monday. And she had texted a few times.

But he wanted to talk to her. He really wanted to see her. And he definitely wanted to kiss her again.

He'd spent the weekend mooning over Emerson like some love-crazed teenager, when he should have been thinking about the bar, his dad's house, his life. He had serious decisions to make and all he could do was obsess over a kiss.

The only thing keeping him from going that extra mile and hitting Send on his cell phone was the unknown. Did she regret the kiss? Jack could tell she'd been into it in the moment. And he sure as hell had been too.

She'd been fairly quiet on the drive home from her parents. Hardly surprising, considering the events of the evening. The reminder of her mother's behavior caused him to exhale a long, frustrated breath. How could she not see how amazing Emerson was?

Even more frustrating was Emerson herself. Jack understood respecting the people who raised you, but Emerson's blatant lack of self-respect was troublesome. Why didn't she defend herself?

His earlier worry morphed into anger. Emerson was awesome and he wanted everyone to know that. Especially her.

He snatched his phone from his pocket once more and punched the send button.

"Hey, Jack," Emerson answered, after two rings. "I—"

But he didn't let her finish. "I want to see you."

The line was disturbingly quiet for a long moment. Jack worked hard to calm his breathing.

Finally, she spoke. Jack thought he heard a bit of humor in her short answer.

"Okay."

Okay? That was easy. He was about to say so when the door of the bar swung open and she appeared, looking professional and beautiful in gray pants and a navy blue sweater. Her auburn curls bounced around her face as she stepped into the bar.

"Here I am," she said with a smile.

Instantly, he relaxed. "That was fast."

She laughed and made her way toward him. "Well,

I was actually on my way over here." He stared at her blankly. "You know, to talk about plans for the bar?"

"Oh. Right!" He met her halfway, by coming out from behind the bar.

"Want something to drink?"

She shook her head. "I'm good," She looked around the room. "Where's Cosmo?"

"He's at home. I didn't think keeping a dog here was the most sanitary thing on the planet."

Her face fell. "Oh. Well, I brought him some treats from the doggie bakery down the street."

Jack stared at the bag she offered, covered in little bones. "There are doggie bakeries?"

"Of course. There are doggie gyms and doggie day-cares, not to mention doggie happy hour. Oh," she said excitedly, clapping her hands together. "You should look into doing something like that. People love it."

Jack ran a hand over his face. "I am not serving a four-legged beast a daiquiri," he said stubbornly.

"Maybe the four-legged beast preferred a beer any-way," she said with a smile. "How was your weekend?"

"I was here all weekend."

"Was it busy? A lot of customers?"

Jack groaned. "Hardly. We really need to turn this place around."

"That's why I'm here." She walked to the closest table, placed the bag she was carrying onto it and reached in-side. "I've been working on the bar all weekend."

He sat at the table with her and raised an eyebrow. "Oh really?"

"Yes. Thanks to me, The Wright Drink is now on Facebook, Twitter, Instagram and Snapchat. I also did some upgrading to your website. Thanks for getting me the access to it, by the way."

She pulled her laptop out of a separate bag and pulled up the website. "Until we clean this place up, do a little redecorating and decide on some events, there's not much I can do with the website. We need photos. Videos would be even better."

Emerson showed him each of the social media platforms. He was impressed to see small followings in each place.

"Wow. You did all of this in a couple of days?"

"Well, I took Saturday off completely, if you must know."

His fingers itched. This moment definitely called for one of his banned cigarettes. "This is really great, Em. I'm on Facebook, but none of those other things. I'm not really a social media kind of guy, so I don't really have the expertise to manage them. Or the time."

"Of course not. I hired someone for you."

"You *what*? Who? When? How much does something like that cost?"

"Don't worry. I have a couple of people who I work with on the social media side of things. Katlyn's really good. And she's inexpensive. But she'll have a ton of social media attention in no time. It's the easiest way to advertise, and it can be cost-effective too."

She really had her stuff together. How could her family not see that?

"Happy, shmoopie?" she asked with a wink.

"No."

"No?" Her face fell. She fumbled with the laptop, toggling between pages. "What don't you like? I was just playing around with this banner on Twitter, but we can certainly change it."

Jack had noticed that, all during her social media spiel she hadn't made eye contact with him. That's when he realized that she might be embarrassed about what had happened between them the other night.

So he grabbed her chair and pulled her closer, forcing her to look up at him.

"I don't like that you've been using work to avoid me."

Her cheeks blushed red. "I haven't been avoiding you." She quickly averted her eyes.

With a light finger under her chin, he tilted her head up so she had to meet his gaze. "Emerson."

"I've been working for you." She gestured toward her computer.

"Are you embarrassed about something?" he asked.

"Such as?"

"You tell me," he countered. She was cute when she was annoyed. Her blue eyes took on a bright crystal color.

"My parents? Well, it's probably too late to get adopted into a new family, as you suggested the other night."

He shook his head.

"The awful photos you saw of me at their house?"

He waited patiently.

"What?" she asked.

With his finger still under her chin, he gently pulled her face closer. "That kiss," he said quietly. He moved his other hand to caress the soft skin of her cheek.

"No, I mean, I, well, I…"

"I really liked it," he filled in for her.

Her lips twitched. "Really?"

"Oh yeah. Did you?"

Her tongue poked out to wet her tempting lips. "Um, that would be a definite *yes*."

He gave a hard nod. "Good. That settles that."

"No, it doesn't. Things are complicated between us." She tried to pull away, but he held firm. "We're lying to everyone. We're pretending to date. I'm helping with your bar. To top it off, you said you're probably going to move out of the area in a month or two. I would be crazy to start anything with you. To kiss you again." But she tilted her head as she said the words.

Jack didn't need more invitation than that. He took her lips for a second time.

Instantly, her lips softened, and he took advantage by moving his mouth over hers. Hungrily, greedily.

She moaned as her arms came up to wind around his neck. He pulled her even closer, unable to get enough of her.

The kiss felt amazing, surreal. He ran his hands through her hair, tangling his fingers in those silky curls. His tongue dove into her mouth, taking the kiss even deeper.

Someone made a guttural sound and he had no idea which of them it was. He ripped his mouth from hers and trailed it down the column of her neck. She obliged by throwing her head back.

But he needed more.

He yanked her up and pulled her onto his lap. She met his gaze, with her eyes dark and full of lust. Threading her hands through his hair, she brought her head down for another satisfying, delicious kiss.

"Excuse me?"

They both started and moved to separate, but Jack was seated in one of the chairs and Emerson was on top of him. Realizing they were more entwined than one of the soft pretzels served at the bar, they both turned toward the voice.

"Am I interrupting something?" A man stood right inside the door, wearing a long black coat over a black suit, and he had an amused grin. He walked down the three steps and his grin got even bigger.

"Xander Ryan," Jack said. His best friend from high school was standing there as Emerson jumped off his lap and adjusted her top, her gaze ping-ponging between the two of them.

"I think one of the last times I saw you in high school, you were in a similar position with Lizzie Demarco."

"Ass," Jack uttered as he stood. But he was grinning from ear to ear. He grabbed Xander in a hug. "Good to see you, man."

"Ohmigod," Emerson groaned. "This is *so* embarrassing." Jack turned back and saw Emerson glance down at her sweater and then run a hand through her hair. He didn't think it was wise to point out that her lips were swollen from their make-out session and her face was flushed. He also imagined that the majority of her lipstick was on his face.

"Hi," she said to Xander, extending her hand.

He shook it—maybe too enthusiastically, Jack observed. "Hey there. I'm Xander, this loser's best friend. We went to high school together."

"Emerson Dewitt. I'm helping this loser whip the bar into shape."

"Hey," Jack protested. Before he could say more, Emerson was grabbing her laptop and other supplies from the table.

"Well, I think we can finish discussing this later. I'll let the two of you catch up."

"Em, wait." But she was already at the front door. "When should we talk again?"

"Um, just text me. We'll work it out." With that, she ran out the door.

"Dammit." Jack needed a drink. Ignoring Xander, he walked to the bar.

"Nice business meeting," Xander said, following Jack.

"Shut up."

"No, really. It's not exactly how we do things at the firm, but to each their own."

"Drink?" Jack held up a bottle of whiskey.

"Wouldn't say no."

Jack filled two glasses and pushed one across the counter, finally taking a moment to give Xander a once-over. His formerly rowdy and mischievous best friend was all grown-up, wearing a tailored suit, with his dark hair short and perfectly in place.

The two of them had played baseball together. Not to mention, they'd constantly gotten into trouble together, as well. But Xander had always been able to talk his way out of any jam.

When his mom had died, Xander sat next to him in the funeral home. He never pushed him to talk about it, which Jack appreciated to this day.

"It's really good to see you." Jack saluted him with his glass.

"You too. Sorry about your dad. And I'm really sorry I couldn't be at the funeral. I was across the country, on business."

He'd sent flowers though. And a mountain of food to the house.

"No worries. Thanks for everything you sent." Jack leaned against the bar. "Xander Ryan, Esquire. Can't believe a real live attorney is standing in my bar."

"Can't believe this is your bar. And I'm not just an attorney. I'm *the* top divorce attorney in the state."

Jack cocked an eyebrow. "You come up with that yourself, or are people aware of your awesomeness?"

Even though they hadn't been in the same room in close to ten years, they had stayed in touch over the years. Phone calls, Facebook, text messages. Being in the same room again didn't feel any different from when they'd been teenagers.

"Everyone is aware of me. But I don't want to talk about me. How about you fill me in on that lovely lady who just ran away from you?"

"Emerson," Jack supplied.

"New girlfriend?"

"No. Yes," Jack remembered. "Sort of." He straightened. "How much time do you have?"

Xander responded with an arched eyebrow. He crossed his arms over his chest and waited. Jack told him the whole story.

"Well," Xander said, and then chuckled. "That's quite the situation you've got yourself in."

"You're no help."

"Sorry, dude, this is uncharted territory. I've seen you with lots of girlfriends. But fake girlfriends? That's definitely a new one. At least Emerson seems cool."

She was more than cool.

"Interesting," Xander said.

"What?"

"That dreamy look you just got. You sure this is all fake?"

"Of course. She's helping me with the bar and I'm helping her out with her family. Especially her mom. She seems to put a lot of pressure on her."

"Isn't that kind of common with mothers and daughters?" Xander asked.

"Not like this. I mean, Emerson is one of the smartest people I've ever met. She started her own business, and you should see how she's been building it up. Plus she's beautiful."

"Uh-huh." A grin broke out on Xander's face.

"What's that about?" Jack asked.

"I've heard you call women hot, sexy and a string of other words. But never beautiful."

Jack shrugged.

"Man, you're in deep already."

Jack had no idea what to say to that. He didn't know if he was in deep, but he was completely aware that he was interested in Emerson Dewitt. He wanted to get to know her more. He wanted to kiss her again.

But there were so many unknowns in his life right now. What would he do with the bar? How long would he stay in Alexandria?

The one thing he did know was that he was damn glad he was in that alley the day she fell out of the window.

He looked to his friend. "Any advice?"

"You've already committed to this fake stuff." He pointed to the table where Jack and Emerson had their earlier make out session. "But what I walked in on today was definitely not pretend. In fact, it looked about as real as it comes."

It felt real, as well. And what was he going to do about that?

Chapter Seven

Almost a week had passed since Xander had uttered those unforgettable words to him.

It looked about as real as it comes.

Jack knew Xander was right. Because in that moment with Emerson on his lap, his arms around her, his mouth against hers, there was no other place he'd rather be.

At least things were less awkward between him and Emerson. Possibly because they hadn't talked about that kiss. Either kiss. Avoidance might be the key to their relationship.

She was at the bar today, armed with paint supplies. At her insistence, Jack had closed the bar for a week. Emerson hired professional cleaners to come in and work their magic. She'd also had him order new light fixtures, fix a few odds and ends, and rearrange some of the tables. Minimal changes and already it felt like a brand-new place.

Not to mention that he'd had a chance to go through

inventory and meet with his dad's accountant. The bar wasn't in great financial shape, but it wasn't quite as bad as he'd originally feared either.

"This paint color is really going to pop. Between it and the new lighting, you'll really see a difference. Everything will be brighter and more inviting. But don't worry, it will still retain that old-school pub vibe."

"The way you rearranged the tables already gives the space some new life."

She shrugged as if it were nothing. "Minor detail."

He grabbed her hand as she started to walk away from him. "It is a big deal, Em. You've done a lot."

"Not really."

"Yes, really." He would make her realize how amazing and talented she was if it killed him. "You're really good at what you do."

That brought a big smile to her face, which was followed by a sweet pink blush. "Most of what event planners do is behind the scenes. Trust me, we always hear if something goes wrong. But when everything runs smoothly, it usually goes unnoticed. It's just part of the job."

She started rifling through one of the bags she'd toted in. "Aha, here they are." She produced four black frames with black-and-white photos inside them. She laid them out on one of the tables.

Jack moved closer to take a look. The first photo was of King Street. Only, something seemed different.

"It's a photo from the year your dad opened the bar," Emerson said. "So is this one." She tapped a purple-painted fingernail at the second frame.

The photo was the front of the bar. "Where did you get these?" he asked.

She smiled. "I found them in that box we noticed in

the corner of your dad's office the other day. He'd already blown them up. I just bought the frames."

Jack studied the next two photos and felt something clench inside his chest. One was a picture of his dad behind the bar, wearing a huge grin, with his hand poised on top of the beer tap. It was such a familiar pose. How many times had Jack looked up at the bar as a child, and there was his dad in that exact position?

But it was the last photo that had the air choking up in his throat. His mom sat on a barstool, with her long legs crossed and angled off the side of the chair. She looked like a pinup girl from the fifties. Next to her was a ten-year-old boy with too-skinny legs, wearing too-high socks, ratty sneakers and a ball cap, and he was grasping a baseball glove. A Shirley Temple with extra cherries was on the bar in front of him. His dad was standing behind the bar with a dish towel flung over his shoulder.

"Do you like them?" Emerson asked, with her voice betraying her nerves.

He still couldn't speak. Jack was moved beyond belief. A myriad of emotions floated over him, and for the life of him, Jack didn't know which one to focus on.

He actually felt tears welling up, but he coughed a couple of times and willed himself to come back to reality.

"Jack?" Emerson asked.

Finally, he turned to her. In a soft and emotional voice, he said, "I love these."

Relief saturated her face. She let out a breath. "Yeah, me too. It's special touches like these that make a place extraordinary. After we paint the walls, I think you should hang them over there." She pointed to one side of the room as he suddenly closed the distance between them. "Whatcha doing?" she asked coyly.

His gaze landed on her mouth. "What do you think I'm doing?"

"I think you're about to ask me about paint samples."

"Not exactly."

"You're wondering if I picked up paint rollers?"

"Definitely not."

He reached for her just as his phone rang. He looked down at it, cringed, pressed a button and then shoved the phone back into his pocket.

Emerson let out a little laugh. "Who was that?"

He frowned. "That was the pushiest bride I've ever met."

The moment was over, and Emerson pushed away from the him, all business once again. "You must not have met many brides then. Trust me, the pushiest wouldn't be calling you. She would be in here, talking about Pinterest boards and accent colors. Why is a bride calling you anyway?" She strolled to one of the tables, where she'd dumped about twenty different bags from the local home-renovation store and began rummaging through them.

"She and her fiancé met at this bar. They want to have a joint bachelor/bachelorette party here. I told them no—"

She dropped a paintbrush and spun around to face him. "Are you for real? Of course they can have it here."

"Are *you* for real? We're not ready for something like that." He waved his hand around to the bar, most of which was covered in drop cloths, since they were going to begin painting today.

She sighed. "Not yet. But we will be. And that's the perfect way to get this place back off the ground. Why didn't you tell me about this earlier?"

"They want the whole place to themselves."

"Even better. Do you have any idea how it will look

on social media when I say the bar is closed for a private event? Exclusive. Desirable," she answered for him. "People will be strolling by on the street and hear the noise, see the party through the windows. This is perfect."

He waved his phone in the air. "Perfect is exactly what Trina wants."

Emerson froze again. "Trina Mitchell?"

"How did you know? You have a psychic side business you aren't telling me about?"

"My best friend, Grace, is planning her wedding. And Grace owes me a favor because I'm helping her out with a different event. Not to mention a million other things from over the years. Let me give her a call."

She whipped her phone out, dialed and was already talking in excited tones before Jack could even protest again.

"It's all set," Emerson said five minutes later. "Two Saturdays from now."

Jack paused in the middle of opening up cartons of painter's tape. "Excuse me? Two weeks? There's no way in hell we're going to be able to do that. Look at this place." The Wright Drink was a pretty large space, as far as bars in Old Town went. "It will take the two of us days to paint everything."

"Oh ye of little faith." There was a twinkle in her eye and Jack had to wonder what she was up to.

As if on cue, the front door of the bar swung open and Emerson's parents and sister entered the bar, with big smiles on their faces.

"The cavalry," Emerson explained with a smile. "I asked a couple of people to come help us today."

"Reporting for paint duty," Amelia said. Her face fell. "Charlie couldn't make it. Sorry."

"No problem," Jack said. "I can't believe any of you are here. Not a fun way to spend a Saturday."

Mr. Dewitt slapped a hand on Jack's back. "Anything to help out Emerson's boyfriend."

Guilt lodged in his throat. Not only was he monopolizing the Saturday of good, hardworking people, but he was lying to them in the process.

"Emerson, what's happening with your hair?" Mrs. Dewitt asked, with a perplexed expression on her face.

Jack took notice. He liked her hair today. For some reason, it was extra curly. She had it piled on the top of her head, in a messy ponytail. Some of the curls had escaped to frame her makeup-free face. She looked natural, beautiful.

Emerson's hand flew to her hair. "Who cares about my hair? We're about to start working."

"I think it looks nice, Em," Amelia said. Making herself at home, she peeked into the bags of paint supplies.

Mrs. Dewitt pointed at her husband. "Give Jack the food, Walt."

Before he could realize what was happening, Mr. Dewitt produced two large bags from the local deli across the street. He peeked inside to find a mountain of sandwiches, chips, fruit, and all of the napkins, utensils and condiments they could need.

"For lunchtime," Mr. Dewitt explained. "We figured we didn't need to bring drinks," he said with a laugh.

"I think I've got you covered," Jack said. "Seriously, this is really generous of all of you."

Emerson waved a nonchalant hand. He wondered if she realized how similar it was to a gesture her mother had made.

"I invited my best friend, Grace, too. She's going to

be late though. She's with one of her brides at an emergency dress fitting."

"I told Grace not to trust that store in Fredericksburg. I knew they'd get it wrong," Beatrice said from across the room, where she was surveying the ancient jukebox.

"You can remind her when she shows up," Emerson said.

Mr. Dewitt engulfed Emerson in a big hug. Then he moved to the back of the bar with Mrs. Dewitt and Amelia as the door opened again and Xander strolled through, wearing a Georgetown Law sweatshirt that had definitely seen better days.

"What are you doing here?"

"I got a call from a certain event planner, saying my considerable talents were needed here."

Jack raised an eyebrow. "Since when do you have painting talents?"

"I have talents the world isn't even ready for…"

Jack was about to throw back a very sarcastic reply when the door opened and an incredibly gorgeous woman with thick black hair ran right into Xander's back.

"Oh excuse me," she mumbled.

But when she came around and faced Xander, something passed over her face. Jack didn't quite understand it. However, he noticed that Xander had gone as still as stone.

"You must be Grace," Jack said to break the ice.

She turned her gaze to Jack and a smile blossomed on her face. The woman was striking. She wore a cherry-red pantsuit with matching heels. Over her shoulder was an incredibly large red tote bag. Jack was pretty sure he'd carried something the same size when he had backpacked around Europe for a year.

"And you must be Jack. I'm so sorry I'm late."

"No problem. We haven't even begun yet." Jack gave Xander a pointed stare, waiting for his friend to introduce himself. Or even to stop ogling Grace.

"This would be my friend Xander. He's here to help too."

Grace gulped. Then she thrust her hand forward. "Nice to meet you, Xander."

He accepted her hand and they shook for a moment. A very long moment. "Hi," Xander finally said. "Do you live here in Old Town?"

Grace ripped her hand from his and clutched her gigantic purse. "Yes, I live with Emerson."

"You seem overdressed for painting."

"I came from work. I was with a bride. I'm a wedding planner."

Xander emitted a snicker, followed by an eye roll. "I'm a divorce attorney."

Silence, thicker and more potent than the paint, filled the air.

Jack stepped forward. "You guys seem to have similar professions," he tried to joke. But something had changed on Xander's face. If Jack wasn't mistaken, it seemed a lot like disappointment.

"Yeah," Xander agreed with a snort. "Couples go to you first and then find me when they come to their senses."

Grace's mouth fell open and she looked like she'd just been slapped.

Emerson had joined Jack at his side.

"Should we throw some cold water on them?" he muttered to her, only half joking. They exchanged a glance, neither seemingly wanting to step in between their two best friends.

Finally, Emerson let out an obvious cough. "Gracie,

thanks for coming." She walked up the steps and retrieved her friend, who offered one last hostile look at Xander over her shoulder.

Grace took in the bar. "This place is fabulous. I can see why Trina and Nick want to have their parties here."

"Nice outfit, Grace," Amelia said with a smile.

"I was with a client." She tapped her oversize bag. "I have a change of clothes."

"Grace, how are you? Emerson said you were having trouble with the wedding dress. You know, I told you about that shop." Beatrice ushered Grace toward the bathroom to change.

"Lovely woman," Xander said under his breath to Jack.

"Shh, she's Emerson's best friend."

Emerson clapped her hands together. "Okay, everybody, time to get this painting party started."

Emerson directed everyone to certain areas of the room. They passed out supplies, cranked up the jukebox and got to work.

They were all working in a good groove for about an hour when the music changed, and a slow, romantic song started. Jack recognized it as one of those overplayed, shmaltzy types of songs crooned by a popular singer that everyone played at their wedding.

He was about to make a joke about it when he noticed Emerson's face had paled. In fact, she was holding her paintbrush in midair.

"I'll change it, Em." Amelia rushed to the jukebox. After Amelia had fiddled around for a few moments, a fast-paced country song began.

What in the world?

"You seem confused."

He turned to find Amelia standing close, studying his face.

"Em didn't tell you what happened with Thad last year, did she?" Amelia asked.

"I've heard plenty of references to last year, but no one has filled me in yet."

Amelia glanced around the room. Everyone was once again busy working on their area of the bar. Someone was singing along, off-key.

"Come on, let's get started."

He followed Amelia to one of the walls, and together they laid out a drop cloth and filled their tin with paint.

"Emerson was engaged to this guy, Thad."

Jack dipped his paintbrush into the tin. "I'm assuming by the use of past tense and the grimace you just offered that the engagement didn't end well."

"Hardly. He backed out of the wedding."

Jack tightened the grip around his paintbrush.

"Emerson was devastated. She had just started her business, and he left her with an overpriced townhouse. For a while, she thought she might have to give up the business and go work in a corporate job to pay the bills. She's getting by now though. Em is very resilient."

He agreed with the last part. Emerson was strong. The only problem was that she didn't always see that trait in herself.

"So that's why she freaked out when she was trying on wedding dresses," he said more to himself.

"She told you about that?" Amelia asked.

Jack paused. A little too long, if the curious look on Amelia's face was any indication. "Uh, right. She told me about it." He needed to keep his lies straight. He couldn't very well admit that he'd only met Emerson because she'd pitched herself out of that window, while wearing the wedding dress.

"The song that I just changed was *their* song." She smoothed paint onto the wall. "Not getting married was bad enough," Amelia continued. "But it was so much more than that to Emerson."

"What do you mean?"

"She felt like she was letting everyone down."

That was ridiculous. Her fiancé had broken up with *her*, and she felt like *she* was letting everyone down? He snuck a glance at Emerson. He knew her well enough by now to tell that the smile plastered on her face wasn't quite reaching her eyes. She was still stuck on the song.

Maybe she was also stuck on her fiancé.

He was about to say something to Amelia when he noticed the twinkle in her eyes.

"What?" he asked.

"I know what you're thinking." She shook her head. "Emerson doesn't have feelings for Thad anymore. That's not what that was about." She pointed at the jukebox.

"What was it about then?"

"Em's hard on herself. It doesn't make any sense to me, because I think she's amazing and I really envy…well, she's a great big sister. But not marrying Thad was a failure to her. And this year has been incredibly difficult."

Wouldn't know it to look at her though, Jack mused.

"She hides it well," Amelia said, as if reading his thoughts.

Every day he seemed to learn more about Emerson Rose Dewitt. Each new thing made his respect for her grow even more. He only wished she could see herself through his eyes.

What she needed was a little time to relax and unwind. And that was exactly what he was going to give her.

* * *

"It looks good. Really, really good." Emerson was surveying the room with her hands on her hips and a satisfied smile on her face. A face that currently had a swipe of paint across the cheek.

He'd just finished taking out multiple bags of trash. He had to admit that Emerson's family had really come through. The place really did look amazing. In fact, it reminded him of when his dad had first opened it. All shiny and new looking.

His mother had helped with the decorating back then. She'd been so proud of it.

"We'll give it the proper amount of time to dry. Then we can continue putting the place back together. In the meantime, we need to get things rolling on the bachelor/ bachelorette party."

"Go out with me tonight."

The words flew out of his mouth. Emerson's head snapped toward him. He couldn't blame her for the shocked expression on her face. He'd surprised even himself.

"Huh?" she asked.

He took a deep breath. "You heard me. Let's go on a date tonight."

She snapped her fingers in front of his face. "Are the paint fumes getting to you?"

You're getting to me. "I feel fine. I just think that we've been doing a lot of work and it would be nice to take my pretend girlfriend out on a real date. Spend some time just hanging out together. You know, relax a little."

She looked at him for a long moment. "You don't have to do that."

He reached over and placed his thumb against the paint

smudge on her cheek. It was dry now. She would need to wash her face to remove it. "I want to."

"But—"

"Emerson, go home, take a shower and put something nice on so we can enjoy a fancy dinner together. Please." He offered her his most cocky grin.

She slapped his arm. "Fine."

He could only hope that going out tonight would be as relaxing as he'd promised her. Because right now being around Emerson Dewitt had the opposite effect. If she was around, he was anything but relaxed.

Chapter Eight

He picked Emerson up at seven o'clock, on the dot. She was waiting outside her townhouse.

Her long black coat was unbuttoned, and from the illumination of the porch light, he could make out a bright turquoise dress that hugged her curves. Her hair looked as if she had freshly washed and styled it; her curls hung softly around her face.

He noticed she'd chosen high heels with a bunch of different straps twisting around her legs. The heels seemed high, yet it did little to get her even close to his height.

"You look amazing," he said, stepping closer.

She bit her lip seductively and slowly brought her gaze up to his. Jack didn't know if that was something they taught to females in a super-secret class, but it got to him every time. He leaned down and brought his lips very close to hers, hovering for several moments, tormenting them both. Finally, he laid a chaste kiss on her lips.

Her perfume emanated toward him, wrapping around all of his senses. She smelled of lavender and honey. It made her that much more tempting. Jack had to move back a step or he would have devoured her right there on the spot.

When he presented her with the bouquet of daisies, a gorgeous smile blossomed on her face. Even in the dwindling light, he could see the utter delight. Funny what a big reaction a little bunch of flowers could produce.

After she quickly ran inside to put the flowers in a vase, she returned and they were off to The Fisherman's King, a posh seafood restaurant at the bottom of King Street, on the edge of the Potomac River.

The great thing about Old Town was the diversity. There truly was something for everybody. You could eat food from all over the world, including Thai, Italian and even Ethiopian cuisine. You could pay a couple of bucks for a meal or drop an entire paycheck.

Because of the variety it had to offer, Old Town drew in people from every walk of life. Everyone from young couples with toddlers in strollers to older couples walking hand-in-hand to flocks of teenagers and people with their dogs roamed the streets.

On one popular corner near the Town Hall and Market Square, guides dressed in Colonial costumes corralled tourists into groups. They would usher them around the historic streets, telling them ghost stories. They'd stop at locations that had hosted George Washington and other famous men who had helped shaped the country.

With so many options, Jack had experienced an hour of panic trying to find the right place to take Emerson. In the end, he'd called Xander, who had suggested The Fisherman's King. Jack had scoffed at first. It took weeks to get a reservation at the restaurant. Especially on a Saturday night. But Xander apparently had an in. He'd represented the owner in his divorce.

After parking in a local garage, they'd walked the short distance. Even with Xander's assistance, they still had to hang out in the bar area for about forty-five minutes, making idle chitchat over cocktails.

Eventually they were shown to their table, in a corner of the restaurant, right next to the windows, which offered an amazing view of the water. Lights glittered off the Potomac River as boats bobbed along in the docks right outside. The Woodrow Wilson Bridge, the drawbridge connecting Alexandria to Maryland, stood majestically in the near distance.

"This is great. Thank you," Emerson said. Her eyes were trained on the window. "Look at the wheel. How pretty."

He glanced across the river, at National Harbor, a recent development in Maryland. There was a large hotel and convention center, shops, restaurants, a casino, and outlets. The place continued to grow each day.

They had constructed a Ferris wheel that was currently lit up in flashy tones of bright pink and blue. Supposedly, the view of the DC area was magnificent from the top of the wheel. Maybe he could take Emerson there some night.

"I'm glad you suggested this. I really needed a break."

She'd put makeup on and somehow whatever she used on her eyes had made them appear even more blue. But Jack could still see that dark circles remained. Not surprising. She had to be exhausted with as much as she had going on. She was doing so much for him, and he imagined that she had other clients that she had to tend to, as well.

"You do so much," he said.

A funny expression crossed her face. "Did my sister say something to you?"

Damn, she was perceptive. "What makes you ask that?"

"I saw you guys talking while you were painting together."

"Maybe we were discussing a TV show. Or a recent bestseller."

She leaned forward. "But you weren't doing either of those things, were you?"

"No. We were talking about you."

"What did she tell you?"

He considered downplaying the conversation, but she deserved to know the truth. "She told me about Thad."

"Right." Her happy expression seemed to deflate, and the glittery blue of her eyes dulled. "That's why you asked me out tonight, isn't it? You felt sorry for me. Be honest."

Before he could say anything, the waiter arrived with their wine. They went through the song and dance of presenting the bottle, uncorking it, and giving Jack the first sip. He had a pretty good sense of wine, even though he was definitely more of a beer man. So he slid the glass to Emerson, who took a sip and announced that it was "awesomesauce." The waiter cringed as he filled their glasses.

Jack took a sip. Emerson was right. It *was* pretty awesomesauce.

They both took a long drink. Suddenly the atmosphere had lost some of its earlier ease.

Emerson put her glass down and leaned forward. "As I was saying before this overpriced bottle of wine appeared, you asked me out because you found out about my ex-fiancé and felt bad for me."

He met her halfway by also leaning into the table.

"No. Emerson, listen to me. I asked you out tonight because I…well, I…"

"Yes?"

"I wanted to spend more time with you."

She scooted backward into her chair and bit her lip. "Really?"

"Yeah, really. I do feel bad about what happened to you. But I don't…pity you or anything."

She gnawed on her lower lip. "That makes one of us."

"It must have really sucked to have to call off your wedding. What an ass."

She emitted a little laugh. "Pretty much. I mean, standing there in my wedding dress and knowing that there were hundreds of people on the other side of the wall… I don't think I've ever been more embarrassed in my life. I certainly hope I'll never be that embarrassed again."

Jack straightened and focused on her. Had he just heard that right? Emerson hadn't only been dumped by her fiancé; if he was understanding her right, that bastard had stood her up at the altar. Actually, bastard wasn't a strong enough word for the coward who could possibly let a woman as amazing as Emerson down.

Tonight was definitely out of the ordinary for her. She'd been out on plenty of dates. She'd even eaten at this particular restaurant before. After all, with its expensive food, snobby waiters and scenic view of the water, it was one of her parents' favorite places.

However, she'd never been out with her pretend boyfriend before. Maybe because she didn't make a habit of acquiring imaginary beaus.

But here they were. Jack cleaned up nicely. He was wearing black slacks and a great tie with a cream-colored sweater over it. Of course, he still didn't quite fit in with the restaurant crowd. How could he when he'd entered the restaurant wearing his sexy leather jacket and sporting the yummiest dark stubble.

He was all dark and brooding, and just delectable. What she wouldn't give to lean over and take a little bite.

When she glanced up at Jack though, his face had become tense.

"Do you need more time with the menu, or are you ready to order?" The tall, thin waiter asked.

"I'll have the halibut special," Emerson said. Jack ordered the same.

Once the waiter was out of earshot, she asked, "Why are you looking at me like that?"

"Em, are you kidding?"

Huh? "I like halibut."

"No. Not the food. We were talking about Thad. I didn't realize that… I mean, I had no idea that he… Are you telling me that this Thad guy left you at the altar?"

Confused, she cocked her head. "I thought you said you talked to my sister earlier."

"I did. But she said he backed out on your wedding. I didn't realize he actually backed out of the church."

Ah, she understood now. He'd assumed that Thad did the decent thing. And true, it *would* have been great for him to call off the wedding when the wedding wasn't actually in progress.

"I'm not sure he ever showed up at the church, to be honest," she emitted a small, humorless laugh. "Not to worry though. He sent a text."

She could see his fingers curl into fists, creating a stark contrast to the tidy white linens, candles and flowers on the table. "You've gotta be kidding me."

"I wish I were."

Her gaze drifted off as she remembered that day. That

horrible, humiliating day. She'd gotten dressed at her parents' house, but once she and her family had arrived at the church, they'd waited in a back room. Her mother kept fluffing her veil and fixing her dress.

Her sister had been absolutely glowing. Besides the fact that Amelia resembled a high-fashion model in her champagne-colored bridesmaid's dress, Charlie had proposed to her the night before, at the rehearsal dinner. He'd gotten up presumably to give a toast to Emerson and Thad. Instead he'd professed his love for Amelia, gotten down on one knee and asked for her hand in marriage.

Everyone in the room had swooned. But Emerson had been pissed. Not that she hadn't been happy for her sister, but it was supposed to be her time. Her wedding. Her rehearsal dinner. She had finally been doing something that made her mother extraordinarily happy. Only, that had been taken away from her too. Of course, Amelia hadn't known Charlie was going to propose, and given what had happened the next day, it didn't matter anyway. But still, after a lifetime of messing up and not doing things her mother's way, couldn't she have that one night to shine?

As they waited at the church the next day, there was a point when her stomach sank. She knew something was off. When Grace had entered the room, carrying Emerson's cell phone and wearing a grim expression, Emerson knew.

"His text said that his heart wasn't into the marriage. He liked me, but he didn't love me."

She felt the heat from Jack's hand before she even realized he'd covered her own. He squeezed lightly. She met his eyes.

"I'm really sorry, Emerson."

"Thanks." She tried to push down the lump forming in her throat but had difficultly. She took a long sip of water. "In the end, I suppose I should be thankful. Thad and I didn't have a lot in common. Of course, I thought that we were a case of opposites attracting."

"What were you, then?"

"Two people who looked great together on paper. The right families, the right schools, the right credentials."

"I didn't realize things like that still mattered."

"For certain people, they do." She removed her hand from his and clasped her fingers together tightly. "The worst part was how much I let down my family." She cast her gaze at the table.

"How can you say that? What does your marriage have to do with your family?"

"It was important to my mama," she whispered. "Mothers love when their daughters get married, and Southern moms, well, amplify that idea by a million."

"Emerson," he began, but she shook her head to stop him.

"I know it probably doesn't make much sense to you."

"Try to explain it," he encouraged.

"I wanted to give my mama this big, beautiful wedding with the perfect poufy wedding dress and a five-tiered cake. I wanted her to have that mother-of-the-bride moment, with all of her friends present. To dance with my dad to their favorite Beatles song. I wanted the picture-perfect wedding day because I knew how much it would mean to her."

Jack narrowed his eyes. "But why? Why did you want to give her that picture-perfect wedding? And why do it if it didn't mean anything to you?"

"There are so many times in my life when I tried to make Mama happy. Dancing and cheerleading and pageants. A dozen other ways. But I would always mess up somehow. I just wanted one time, one day, one moment, of being in the spotlight for the right reason."

"Hmm." Jack rubbed a hand along his jawline. "Bet your sister didn't make it any easier."

"I love Mia." Emerson heard the defensiveness in her voice.

Jack leaned forward. "Of course you do. It still must have been hard to have your little sister outshine you at every turn."

It felt like someone had just removed their hand from Emerson's mouth and she could finally breathe. "I don't want to seem catty or mean-spirited."

Jack let out a gruff laugh. "Trust me, Em, that's the last thing I would ever say about you. Relationships are complex. It's okay to have multiple feelings about a person."

She considered his words for a very long moment. Then finally, she let loose. "It was hard. It still is. Dammit," she added for emphasis.

"Sometimes I feel so exhausted," Emerson continued. "I have to try extra hard all of the time. Either I do something my mama wants me to do and she thinks I did it wrong, or I do something she doesn't support entirely and thrive without her approval. I can't seem to win."

"Why would you want to?" Jack asked. She could see the sincerity in his eyes. "Look at all of the amazing things you have done in your life."

"They weren't the things that impressed Mama. I was never quite good enough. I wasn't Amelia." She finished with a laugh that had absolutely zero humor to it.

"I mean, sure, Amelia was a cheerleader, but it's not like cheerleading ever won her any scholarships." She pointed at Jack. "Did you know that I received multiple scholarships for both academics and soccer?"

"No kidding."

"Amelia went to the college my parents loved. Big deal. She's working in Mama's store now. Um, she studied marketing. Why isn't she using her degree?"

Emerson knew her sister loved weddings and enjoyed working with brides and their families. But she also knew that Amelia wasn't 100 percent happy with her chosen profession. She'd been hinting at her discontent for a while now.

"Ugh." Emerson felt horrible. She rubbed at her temples.

"What is it?" Jack asked.

"I feel awful, being so critical of my sister."

He studied her for a long moment. "You've been compared to your sister your whole life, and instead of begrudging her, you love her. It's so clear to anyone who sees the two of you together."

"One day I might believe that." How she truly wished she would.

"I hope I'm there to see that day."

Emerson took a long, fortifying drink of wine. "There's something else." She fidgeted in her seat. "I've never told anyone this."

Jack didn't press. He waited patiently.

"I don't think I even loved him very much. I think… maybe it was the idea of him?" She sighed. "He snored. And he was kind of snobby. He refused to go to the movies because he said all movie theaters were dirty. Plus he told his mother that he went to church every Sunday, but I don't think he even knew where the closest church was." She was so upset, she knocked over her wineglass. Bright red liquid spilled across the crisp white linen.

A busboy rushed over to take care of the toppled wineglass.

"Thank you," she said to the busboy. Then she turned

her attention back to Jack. "I mean, who did he think he was? Screw him," she yelled a little louder than she should at a fancy restaurant. "Thad thought he was *so* great and *so* charming. You know what though? He wasn't all that."

The maître d' also made his way toward the table. "Miss, is everything okay?"

"Oh yes," Jack said with a twinkle in his eye. "She's having a long, overdue epiphany."

"As cathartic as that may be, we do have other guests here tonight."

Emerson glanced around the restaurant and found that every pair of eyes was trained on her, watching her outburst. Some sat with their mouths hanging open, while others actually appeared to be amused with her theatrics.

All she could think was how her mother would disown her if she saw this. Particularly because this was one of her favorite restaurants. What would everyone think? And that thought actually made her laugh.

Not just laugh. Hysterical sounds escaped her body as tears ran down her cheeks.

"Sir, I'm very sorry, but I must insist you and your companion settle down."

The maître d' didn't even attempt to address Emerson. Probably thought she'd completely lost it at this point. She couldn't be sure she hadn't. But if this was losing it, it sure did feel good. Another belly laugh rolled through her and ended with a loud snort, which only made her laugh more.

"Sir, please." The maître d's gaze darted from table to table. "If you can't tone down your conversation, we do have a lovely table in a more secluded area of the restaurant."

"More secluded?" Jack asked. He rolled his eyes. "Why don't we just leave then?"

"If that's what you want to do."

Emerson was pretty sure Jack's suggestion had been a hypothetical. Nevertheless, the maître d' had snapped his fingers and the busboy appeared. They began stripping the table.

Jack stood and reached for his wallet, but the maître d' shook his head, seemingly more intent to just get them out of the restaurant and away from the normal patrons.

"Our food?" Jack asked.

"Not to worry. I'll cancel the order. Consider the wine complimentary." He gestured toward the entrance. Or, in this case, the exit. "This way, please."

Emerson thought she'd go to the restaurant tonight and get a great meal. Instead she got something much greater.

A little closure.

Chapter Nine

Since they'd forfeited their four-star dinner—all her fault, Emerson had to admit—Jack asked her what she was in the mood for. So they picked up large, juicy cheeseburgers, with two sides of fries, and then Jack drove them a little ways from Old Town.

She enjoyed being in the car with him. Her window was cracked, and the cool night air felt amazing against her skin. She leaned her head against the glass and searched for stars above the twinkling city lights.

She lost track of where they were heading as she ran over all the things she'd said tonight. All of the things she'd thought.

Jack switched on the radio and found the local country station. One of her favorite songs came on. She smiled.

Her favorite food. Her favorite song. And Jack was very quickly becoming one of her favorite people.

With Jack, everything felt different. She could say things to him that she wouldn't dare utter to another soul.

She gnawed on her lip as she considered the situation. When she was with him, she felt…whole. That wasn't quite right. Maybe it was more that she felt like herself. No explanations. No apologies.

Suddenly it hit her.

When she was around Jack, she felt good enough. She never felt as though she had to make excuses for herself. She just was.

Maybe she could be herself with Jack. Perhaps Emerson Rose Dewitt *was* enough.

He put the car into Park at the top of a hill. There was no one else around. No other cars, people, houses. Nothing. It was dark and secluded and absolutely…romantic.

Perfect.

The radio continued playing softly in the background as Emerson leaned her head back against the seat and closed her eyes.

"Did we just technically get kicked out of a restaurant?"

She heard the rustle of the food bags. The aroma of onions and fries wafted through the confined space of the truck. Jack rolled the windows down about halfway. It was still chilly outside, but with each week the temperature rose higher and higher. Summer would be here before they knew it.

"I believe we did."

She opened her eyes and watched as Jack winked at her and stuck a fry in his mouth. Naturally, it drew her attention to those tempting lips. Those lips that had now been on hers twice. Maybe she wanted them to be on hers again. Maybe she wanted to continue her uncharacteristic behavior and just make out right in this truck. After all, what was one more crazy thing when she'd already done so many this evening?

When she finally ripped her eyes away, she noticed that he was grinning at her. No doubt, he knew exactly what she was thinking.

"What are you thinking?"

He was clearly psychic.

But what was she supposed to say? The truth? That she wanted him? That she was on a high from revealing her past to him tonight and wanted to keep the feeling going by ripping his clothes off?

Instead she unwrapped her burger and took a big, juicy bite. Not as satisfying as biting into Jack, but it would have to do.

"I really appreciated you taking me out tonight. The whole routine—the flowers, getting a reservation at that fancy restaurant."

"But?" he asked.

"But I prefer this—a picnic under the stars, a burger and fries. Fancy and polished is not what I crave now."

His eyes raked over her in one sexy, seductive grin. "Oh yeah? What do you crave?"

You. "Now I crave comfort and ease."

He nodded. "You never cease to surprise me."

Emerson looked out the windshield, taking in the setting. To find a quiet area like this, not far from Old Town, was definitely a hidden gem.

"I used to come here in high school."

"Really? But it's so private…oh." Emerson laughed as she realized just what he'd come here in high school to do. "Was this your secret make-out spot?"

He chuckled. "I may have brought a girl or two here." He ate more of his burger and washed it down with a big swig of soda. "But I also used to come up here to be by myself. Take some time away."

He was looking out the windshield, staring out at the

darkness. Even from the side, she could see he'd clenched his jaw. She reached over and gently touched it.

She threw his question back at him. "What are you thinking?"

He opened his mouth, but no words came out. Instead it was as if he had made a decision. He turned to her with a wry grin. "About how great you were back at the restaurant."

Emerson knew he was lying, but she let it go. For now.

"Great, sure. That's one way to put it."

He laughed. "It was. You were amazing. It was good to see you finally realize how messed up that Thad guy was."

He truly was. She'd spent so much time over the last year blaming herself for the humiliating breakup. Like she'd somehow not been good enough for Thad to go through with their marriage. When in reality, it was ridiculous to blame herself at all. Thad was the scoundrel.

Her phone went off. She dug it out of her purse and cringed.

"Let me guess," Jack said. "Your mother?"

"Oh yeah," she said as she declined the call. Almost immediately, a text message popped up.

Emerson, call me.

With her mom, the shorter the text message was, the more pissed off she was. She showed the screen to Jack.

"You think she found out about your outburst in The Fisherman's King?"

Emerson nodded.

"Who do you think told her?" he asked, stretching his arm across the seats.

"Who knows?" She switched her phone to Silent and threw it back in her purse. "Who cares?"

She considered her burger, but she was no longer hungry. She wrapped it up and nestled it back in the bag.

"I realized something tonight. I spent a year mourning the end of a relationship that wasn't all that great to begin with."

Jack remained quiet. He began to massage her shoulder, offering support. That small gesture meant so much to her.

Some of that defiance from the restaurant began to surface again. "He was lucky to have me."

"Damn straight."

"I'm too good for him. I'm…" She didn't know what else. She only knew one thing. She was so done with Thad and that part of her life.

Jack's hand stilled on her shoulder. She turned to face him.

Other than the music playing on the radio, the only sounds were that of crickets and a light wind blowing through the trees. Moonlight filtered into the truck, highlighting Jack's handsome face, with its strong jawline and angles.

There were things that were up in the air in her life at the moment. Aspects that weren't ideal. None of that mattered at this second though. It didn't seem to matter what she didn't have or what she hadn't done correctly. Right now, it was about her. About want.

And Emerson knew there was one thing she wanted very badly.

Emerson climbed over to his seat, practically sitting in his lap, and framed his face with her hands. He met her gaze full on as she leaned in to kiss him.

Finally.

It took less than a second for Jack's arms to encircle her, pulling her closer. She heard one of the food bags fall to the floor.

She opened her mouth, welcoming his tongue as it mingled with hers.

Emerson had no idea how long they kissed. It could have been a couple of minutes or a couple of hours. She only knew that she wanted it to last forever.

Finally, they separated. Jack ran his thumb over her bottom lip. When his hand fell to the seat, she licked her lips and delighted when his gaze flew to that spot.

She giggled. "You have to add me to the list of girls you've made out with here."

He ran a hand over her hair, twisting one of her curls around his finger. "You are at the top of the list."

"Because I'm the most recent?"

His jaw ticked as his eyes darkened. He'd grown serious and the air in the truck felt heavy with an emotion she didn't quite understand. Or maybe, she just wasn't ready to acknowledge it. He shook his head at her question.

Jack sat back and rolled his window all the way down. A breeze whistled through the trees, entered the cab of the truck and shifted her hair around her head. The temperature was still a bit cool. She loved how the crispness of the air felt against her cheeks.

The radio began playing a slow, melodic song. She turned up the volume, closed her eyes, and began swaying back and forth.

"Come on." Jack's voice was gruff and sexy as hell.

She opened her eyes languidly to find that Jack had slid out of the truck. Then he reached back in and pulled her outside. Instantly, she was in his arms. His strong arms cocooned her as he brought her body against his.

She didn't care if the moment was like something out

of a movie. Because Emerson was falling for it. She was falling for *him*.

For real.

He swayed from side to side, moving her body with his, around the grassy field, as the song played from the truck.

"You're a good dancer," she commented. "You probably did this with all of those hundreds of girls in high school."

He raised his eyebrows. "Hundreds, huh? Maybe only like ninety-nine."

She hit him lightly on the chest. He covered her hand with his and held it there. Over his heart.

They continued to move together to the music, gazing into each other's eyes. One song rolled into another.

She didn't know when, but at some point they began to kiss. Lightly, so lightly, at first. Her arms wound around his neck. His lips trailed along her jawline and she shivered.

"Cold?" he asked, with his voice already sounding husky.

How could she be anything but blazing hot when she was in his arms?

"No," she replied. Feeling bold from everything that had happened that night, she said, "Touch me, Jack."

Instantly, his hands traveled down her sides, and back up again. They brushed past her breasts and she shivered. His lips came to hers again, sweeping her away into the passion of the kiss.

"Em, is this something you want to do? I mean, is this okay?"

How cute was he? Big, bad Jack Wright had just gotten tongue-tied. Over her. Because of her.

"I want you, Jack. Now. Here."

"You're sure?"

She nodded. "Oh yes."

He quickly made his way to the truck and rummaged in the back seat. After returning with a plaid blanket, he fluffed it out and spread it on the ground.

Emerson glanced around. They'd been in this spot for at least a half hour, with no other signs of life. Still, they were outdoors. In public. Never in her life had she made love in such an open environment. The thought was both scary and empowering.

In any case, she wanted Jack far too badly to even think about climbing back into the truck and driving to one of their houses. She needed him right now.

He knelt on the blanket and reached out a hand to her. The gesture was so romantic that she almost started to cry. Instead she stepped to him and took his hand, noticing how his large hand dwarfed hers.

Standing over him, she leaned down and kissed him. Her hair fell, curtaining his face. Then she joined him in a kneeling position.

They were on even ground.

She could feel moisture under the blanket. An owl hooted in one of the nearby trees. The wind continued to lightly blow around them.

He framed her face with his hands and forced her to meet his gaze. "You are so beautiful, Emerson. Inside and out."

His words humbled her. "Oh Jack."

"Shh." He pressed a finger to her lips. "I want to look at you."

"You've been doing that all night."

He shook his head. "This is different. This is just us. For us."

Another gust of wind, stronger this time, blew around

them. She felt her nipples harden in response. Or maybe that was due to Jack's intense stare. He continued to take her in, as if she were the only woman on Earth. The only woman he'd ever seen. Like she was special. Like she was enough.

"Kiss me," she said.

He did and she melted into it. When his tongue found its way into her mouth, she scooted even closer to him.

Her hands began to run over his strong chest. He was so hard, so masculine. She delighted in feeling all of his muscles and knowing he had the strength to hold her up.

She ripped her lips from his and pressed sweet kisses to his neck, before lightly nibbling his earlobe. A sound of pure delight escaped his lips and she smiled against his skin.

Feeling powerful and bold, she leaned back and reached for the bottom of her dress. She bit her lip as she considered for one second. But this was right. Everything about this moment felt real.

She inched the dress up and over her head until she was kneeling in front of him in nothing but the matching blue lacy bra and panties she'd chosen to wear that night. His dark eyes dimmed to practically black as they trailed up and down her body.

She attempted to take off her heels, but she got stuck. She told herself it was due to all of the intertwining straps and not the fact that she'd suddenly gotten a case of nerves. In the end, she decided to just leave them on.

Jack reached out and trailed a finger over the top of her bra. Her chest was rising and falling rapidly, causing the cups of her bra to overflow with her breasts.

But she wasn't done yet. She yanked his sweater over his head and loosened his tie until she could remove that, as well. Then she began undoing the buttons of his shirt, thrilled to see that her fingers were calm and steady. This was what she wanted.

When she pushed his shirt off his broad shoulders and to the ground, she inhaled sharply. Damn, he was gorgeous.

She couldn't wait. She pressed her hands against his pecs and ran them down to the waistband of his pants. He sucked in a breath.

Their eyes met. A moment passed between them. Then, completely in sync, they grabbed for each other.

Hands were everywhere. Their mouths fused and then explored every inch they could get to. Nothing was off-limits.

Jack cupped her breasts before leaning down to take her nipple into his mouth. The combination of his hot mouth, the cold wind and the lace against her sensitive skin was delightfully unbearable. Her head fell back and she moaned. He unhooked her bra and covered her naked breast with his mouth, his tongue, his teeth.

As he gave the same attention to her other breast, her hand went on its own adventure over his abs and to the zipper of his pants. She pulled it down and snuck her hand inside. Finding what she wanted, she cupped the length of him.

Jack shivered, and a very raw, primal sound slipped out of his mouth.

"Emerson," he said, with a raspy, desperate voice.

"I know, Jack, I know."

He laid her down on the blanket, cupping her head as he did so. The blanket wasn't the softest in the world. It was scratchy and stiff. Some kind of bird or night creature was making a very strange noise. But none of that mattered, because Jack removed his boxer briefs and then her panties. When he covered her body with his, the only thought in her head was of him.

He kissed her deeply. Their tongues entwined in a seductive dance. She grabbed for him, attempting to pull him even closer. She was more than ready for him, wanted him.

"Yes?" he asked.

"Oh yes," she whispered.

Jack reared back, reaching for his discarded pants. He fumbled in the pocket until he pulled out a foil packet. After quickly sheathing himself, he returned to her. Braced on his arms, he towered over her, his eyes serious.

He positioned himself between her legs, pausing to kiss her again. Kissed her long and hard. It felt like he was pouring everything of himself into it. She was so enthralled by it that she almost didn't realize he was entering her at the same time.

He filled her completely as their lips stayed fused together. He captured her gasp of pleasure with his mouth. His arms shook as he pushed in even farther.

Her legs opened wider for him and her arms circled his back, holding on for dear life as he began to move inside her.

This was what it was to be connected to another person. To be intimate. To be adored.

Their bodies moved together as if they had done this countless times. As if they were made for each other.

His arms came around her as he began to move faster, harder. She didn't hear the radio or the night noises, because the only sound filling her ears was Jack's voice, saying her name.

She knew he was getting closer to the ultimate release and could feel her body readying for the same thing. Their hold on each other tightened as stars began to shine behind her eyes. And right there, on the ground in a secluded field, they came together, as one, at the same time.

They stayed just like that for a long time. Wrapped tightly around each other, breathing heavily.

Jack kissed her. Once. Twice. And then another soul-pouring kiss as they stayed connected in the most primal of ways.

Vulnerable. She felt utterly and completely exposed. Not only because of their current state of undress. She felt naked from the inside too.

They held each other, just like that, at the top of a hill, in the darkness, and Emerson knew that nothing in her life would ever be the same.

Chapter Ten

"I am beat," Emerson said to the empty room as she collapsed onto the couch.

It had been a long two weeks. She was up to her eyeballs in events. Two new clients signed on this week. She would be busy through the rest of the year. Between signing contracts, meeting with customers, inspecting event spaces and working on those events she already had in the works, she'd been putting in extremely long days.

She'd never been so grateful for her short commute. Although, after a day like today, the walk from the first floor to her upstairs apartment, had felt like climbing Everest.

She hated to complain about work. Ever since she started her company, she decided that she would be grateful for any work that came her way. Still, it might be time to bring someone else on. At least a part-time employee would help.

"I bet you're tired."

She jumped at the sound of Grace's voice. "I didn't realize you were home."

"Maybe because you haven't been here much this week."

There was nothing accusatory in Grace's tone, yet Emerson felt guilty nonetheless. She'd been spending long hours working. Besides preparing Jack's bar for the upcoming bachelor/bachelorette extravaganza, she was spending a lot of time with Jack.

If the sun was up, she was in complete event-planner mode.

But when the sun went down and the stars came out, that's when she forgot about everything work-related and finally came alive.

It was all thanks to Jack.

They'd spent a lot of time at his house. Sometimes he cooked her dinner, and other times they ordered in. She really didn't have a preference, so long as the night ended in his bed.

Or on the living room floor, as it happened just last night, she thought with a smile.

"What's that grin for?" Grace plopped down next to her on the couch. "You look…hmm…satisfied."

Emerson hit her with a throw pillow. "I'm sorry I haven't been around much lately. Work has been nutso. But all good stuff. Lots of new clients and events."

Grace grabbed the pillow and stuck it behind her head. She scooted down and threw her legs onto the oversize ottoman they used as a coffee table.

"It's okay. I've been busy with work myself. Did you get my email about the bachelor/bachelorette party this weekend?"

Emerson nodded. "Sure did. I replied right before I

came up tonight. Don't worry. Everything is going to be perfect."

"What about with you?" Grace asked. "Is everything perfect?"

Pretty close.

Emerson sat up straight. The silent admission surprised her. Perfection. After a life of never getting close to even being mediocre, this was new and uncharted territory.

She turned to Grace, whom she was surprised to see frowning.

"Jack makes you happy," Grace said matter-of-factly.

Emerson's face grew hot; she knew she was blushing. "I believe someone in this room told me to go for it."

"I was just thinking like maybe a fun little fling. Not spending every day together."

"We don't spend *every* day together." Did they? They'd definitely had a lot to do at the bar, preparing it for the reopening, which would kick off with the bachelor/bachelorette party.

Her phone went off. She could see it on the ottoman, next to Grace's glittery purple-painted toenails. It was a text from Jack.

Apparently Grace noticed, as well. She lifted a perfectly shaped eyebrow in a very what-did-I-just-tell-you arch.

Emerson sighed. "I thought you would be happier. You love romance and happy endings and all that."

"True." Grace dragged out the word and tapped a finger to her lips. "It's just that I'm worried there won't be a happy ending in this case. That there can't be one."

Emerson swallowed a lump the size of the Capitol dome. Her friend was right. She'd been so busy the last couple of weeks that she forgot about the big picture.

She'd been having way too much fun enjoying the small picture, which involved working a fulfilling job during the day, and being in Jack's arms and bed at night.

Jack was only in her life because…well, because they'd made a deal, an arrangement. They weren't even dating.

Although, it sure did feel like they were. She definitely wasn't pretending when she was with him, and she would bet her own life that he wasn't either.

Even if they hadn't talked about it lately, Jack's future was up in the air. He'd been honest and up-front about that since day one. They were preparing the bar to look good for business. Or for a new owner.

The latter choice meant Jack would leave town. Leave *her*.

Purposefully, she avoided Grace's gaze.

"Oh Em, don't be upset." Grace grabbed her hands and squeezed. "I'm sorry."

"You have nothing to be sorry for. You're speaking the truth and we both know it. I've backed myself into a corner." The words tasted coppery as they rolled off her tongue.

Grace wore her heart on her sleeve and Emerson could tell that her friend knew she'd upset her. She tried to offer a smile, but knew it wasn't enough.

"What can I do?" Grace asked. "I didn't mean to rain on your parade. I have to fix this."

"How about some wine? And popcorn? And a really funny movie, so we don't have to think about anything but laughing."

Grace gave her one last once-over. Apparently appeased, she grinned. "Yes to all of the above. I'll get the wine and make the popcorn. You pick the movie."

"And don't forget about the comfy clothes," Emer-

135

son called to her friend's retreating back. "Yoga pants are essential."

"You don't have to tell me twice," Grace yelled from the kitchen.

But she knew that comfy yoga pants and some popcorn weren't going to settle her restless mind. Emerson berated herself. Just when she'd let her guard down and had really begun to feel good with a man, reality came charging back in to step on her popcorn.

Now she had to deal with the possibility that had always been around. She'd just thrown a blanket over it.

Although, maybe Jack wouldn't leave. Maybe he would change his mind. After all, they'd been working so hard on the bar. If he saw how great the party went and how much potential there was in the bar, he might be persuaded to stick around.

She would just have to make sure that every single thing went as smoothly as possible. Not just for the bar.

But for her heart, as well.

Jack hadn't been this nervous since he'd stepped out to bat during his first minor league game. Just like then, his palms were sweating, his pulse was racing and he could feel the adrenaline coursing through his veins.

He paced the floor of the bar, trying to release some of his nervous energy. A lot was riding on tonight. He'd never thrown any kind of event like this party, and all he could do now was hope and pray everything went as smoothly as Emerson promised it would.

It was almost 'go time.' The happy couple and one hundred of their closest friends would be here any minute.

He hoped they had enough of everything. He'd hired some new bartenders and waiters since his father's payroll had been mostly empty, except for Oscar. Speaking of Oscar, he'd been a huge help when it came to the nitty-gritty of supply and food ordering.

But maybe there was something else they hadn't thought of. Maybe Trina and Nick would hate what they had done with the place. This whole thing would be a lot easier to deal with if he'd gotten more shut-eye. He'd had a hell of a time sleeping the night before.

He wasn't sure he wanted to admit that the insomnia may have had something to do with his missing bed companion. They'd worked hard on decorating the bar until about eleven o'clock, the night before. Then Emerson opted to sleep in her own bed.

He'd said he didn't have any problem with that.

He may have been lying.

The truth was he missed her. He missed the way she smiled at him. He missed the way she looked when she was all curled up next to him, with moonlight falling across her face.

Moonlight? "Christ," he mumbled while scrubbing a hand over his face.

He took stock of the bar. It really did look amazing. Emerson insisted The Wright Drink display the proper amount of local DC-area pride. She claimed it would make patrons feel more at home. She'd hung pennants and other signage for the local sports teams. Not to mention, she'd gotten ahold of a signed jersey from one of the Nationals players. It was now proudly being displayed in a glass case, with an accompanying autographed baseball next to it.

Besides the new paint, better lighting, and rearranging most of the furniture, Emerson had gone to town decorating for the party. There were balloons in every corner and signs with the couples' names. She'd brought in even more lighting in the form of centerpieces; intricate candle displays added a romantic ambience. Plus, she'd had a friend of hers build a small stage in one of the back corners. She'd set up a karaoke machine for tonight, and encouraged Jack to keep it around for future celebrations.

Now he just needed to see Emerson. He needed her to help calm his anxiety over tonight's event.

He realized something at that moment. He was nervous because this bar meant something to him. He was also coming to realize that a certain auburn-haired event planner had snuck into his heart.

Huh. Something to consider.

Just then she waltzed into the room, holding her phone between her raised shoulder and her ear. She was carrying her iPad, and her eyes were scanning the screen.

"Fine, fine. I have to run." With that, she removed the phone, sighed and flipped the lid of her iPad shut.

"You look frustrated," Jack observed. "Who was that?"

Emerson tucked her phone back into the pocket of her black pants. "That was one Beatrice Carlyle Dewitt."

Ah. "Your mom. Wishing us well tonight?"

Emerson snorted. "Not exactly. She wanted to ask me what I was wearing to the anniversary gala." She used air quotes when she said gala.

"It's a gala now?" he asked, amused.

"Everything at my mother's house is a gala." She said.

"Are you planning it for her?"

She looked like he'd just thrown her drink in her face. "Are you serious? Do I look like I have a death wish?"

He laughed. He did that a lot around her. It was nice to be able to relax with someone.

"Was she happy with your outfit choice?"

"Have you met my mother? Has she ever not had an opinion that she simply must share with me." She coughed and stuck her nose up in the air as she took on her mother's Southern accent. "Emerson Rose, you simply cannot wear that dress to this party. It's far too audacious. You really should wear something black. Simple. Sophisticated." She stuck her tongue out. "Blah. I wear black when I work events. Not when I'm being social. *Bor-ing*."

Again, he laughed. "I'm sure you'll put your own spin on it." He clapped his hands together. "On to more exciting things, like the kick-ass event you planned for *me*. I made the specialty cocktails you suggested, ordered all the food on your list. What else can I do?"

She did a little spin and narrowed her eyes as she took in every inch of the bar. She walked to some of the tables, straightening chairs that were already perfectly straight.

When she returned to him, she grinned. "I think we're ready."

"Not quite," he said. "Aren't we missing a certain wedding planner?"

"Grace has been texting me every couple of minutes, for the last two hours." She took out her phone to show him. "We just went over everything this morning. I've got this. Anyway, she's working a wedding tonight. She often helps set up bridal showers and bachelorette parties for her clients. Unless it's something really big or extreme, she doesn't usually show up. At least, not for the whole thing."

Jack tapped her phone. "And yet she keeps texting you."

"She's not here, but she cares about her bride and groom. She just wants to make sure everything is going well." Emerson glanced up when the bell she'd added above the door chimed. "Showtime." The door opened and a parade of people entered.

"Oh it looks fabulous." Trina Mitchell jumped up and down excitedly. "Even better than the day we met." With that, she jumped up on a man—presumably the fiancé— and planted her lips on his. Jack hadn't met the guy yet. Emerson had handled all of the meetings.

"Look at the sign, babe. Just for us." Trina was now darting around the bar, taking in all of the details, as a barrage of men and women paraded in. Many of the women wore sashes and tiaras, while the men were dressed for a night on the town.

"Ooohhh look at these tiny cocktail napkins with our names. Ohmigod, our names are being projected on the walls and floors. I love that. Whose idea was that? And look, look. Sweetie pie, it's a specialty cocktail." Trina made a noise and Jack wasn't sure if it was a squeal or a scream.

Emerson leaned in and whispered. "See, snookums, I told you that would be a big hit."

"You do have skills, baby cakes."

It seemed to take no time at all for the music to start blasting out of the jukebox, people to get out on the dance floor and the specialty cocktail to start flowing. Jack barely had a moment to take in the scene. Between watching his two bartenders serving up drinks and the waitstaff replenishing food, he almost missed Emerson running around, taking care of every other little detail.

Of course, he was having a hard time keeping his eyes off her. She was wearing tapered black pants and a loose-fitting black blouse. Her hair was pulled back, showing off her sparkly earrings and a pretty little silver necklace with a heart pendant. Nothing about her outfit should make a man's heart stop, and yet... Something about her made him do a double take every time she flew by.

When he did get a moment to really observe her in action, he was impressed. She was fast, efficient and pleasant. She kept to the edges of the room, but was always there when someone needed something. The waiters, bartenders and partygoers all seemed to enjoy speaking with her. She had a way about her that got her point across, while being cheerful and approachable.

He certainly wasn't an expert, but Jack would guess that Emerson was one heck of an event planner.

"Bye, cupcake."

Jack turned in time to see Nick kiss his fiancée. He knew the guys were taking off for a cigar bar. But the ladies were sticking around all night. While Jack was definitely happy to see The Wright Drink hopping again, he was happy to get a bit of a reprieve, with half of the guest list leaving.

Trina launched herself at Nick, as if he'd just told her he was heading to Mars and wouldn't be back for ten years. "I'll miss you, lovey." She plastered his face with kisses. Despite the men in the room making catcalls and throw-up sounds, Nick seemed perfectly content to let Trina shower him with affection.

Once the men were out the door, the ladies filled up their drinks again and hit the dance floor. Jack found himself laughing as he watched the shenanigans.

"Quite the party," Xander said. He'd arrived right as the other men had been departing.

"Yeah. Emerson did an amazing job. Look at this place."

Xander perused the scene. "Are you turning The Wright Drink into an all-female bar? Because I could be down with that."

Jack threw a penis straw that had been abandoned on the bar at him. Xander picked it up, studied it and then quickly threw it back. "Ugh."

"Would you like a specialty cocktail?" Jack asked with a twinkle in his eye.

"Tempting, but how about a beer?"

"Suit yourself."

"And where is Miss Emerson?"

"Right here." Emerson came up behind Xander and wrapped her arms around his waist, squeezing tightly.

"Not that I mind, but what was that for?" Xander asked.

"You helped us paint this place. That means that you helped this whole party happen, and I appreciate it."

Xander wrapped his arm around her shoulders and brought her to his side. He placed a kiss on the top of her head.

Even though the kiss was short and chaste and completely friendly, Jack felt his heart rate rising. He didn't like seeing Emerson with another guy. Even Xander.

He came out from behind the bar.

"Hey, all he did was paint for a couple of hours." He jerked a thumb at Xander. "I painted, cleaned, moved furniture, changed lights."

"Poor baby," Emerson said with a laugh in her voice. She broke away from Xander and went up on tiptoe so she could press a kiss to one of his cheeks and then the other. "You did an amazing job too. Thank you."

"That was all I asked." He motioned to one of his bartenders. "Hey, Scott, you guys good back there?"

"Absolutely. Take a load off. We got this."

"Drink?" he asked Emerson. "I think you deserve a break too."

"Sure. Sounds good. I might as well try this cocktail everyone is raving about."

"She says with pride." Jack winked at her before dashing behind the bar. He grabbed a beer for himself and a cocktail for Emerson. With Xander, they moved to a corner away from the dancefloor, taking over one of the high cocktail tables Emerson had insisted he needed in order to create levels. Now that he saw them, he had to agree with her. It added dimension to the bar.

The three of them enjoyed their drinks as much as they could over the volume of the music. Eventually, Emerson pushed her cocktail toward the center of the table. "Well, I should be getting back to work."

"Back to what?" Xander asked. "Isn't the party in full swing?"

She smiled. "Yes, but there are always details to check and double-check. How's it going in the kitchen? Are the bartenders okay?" she said, ticking the items off her fingers. "Not to mention that we arranged transportation for the end of the night, and I want to give the car company one last call to confirm."

"You make me tired, Emerson Dewitt," Xander said jovially. "But I have to admit that I've been in here a million times and it has never looked quite this good. You did a really amazing job."

She reached across the table and squeezed his hand. "Thank you. That means a lot." Emerson stood up and both men followed suit. "However, my work is never done."

"Hey," Jack said, joining in. "I've worked hard too. This is my bar after all."

Xander scoffed.

"What?" Jack asked.

Xander threw his arm around Jack's shoulder. "Oh yeah, it's *his* bar until he hightails it out of here again."

Jack laughed at first. But then he noticed Emerson, who seemed to deflate right in front of his eyes. Her shoulders sank, her face fell and her gaze suddenly found the ground incredibly interesting.

He felt like a world-class heel.

They'd just spent almost every day together, over the last couple of weeks. He didn't want to assume anything, but he was fairly confident that Emerson had feelings for him. After all, he'd developed them for her.

The realization struck him right in the gut. He didn't know why he was even surprised. He never would have slept with her if he hadn't felt something for her. And he never would have even asked to take her out if he hadn't.

Actually, it probably went back even further than that. Wasn't that strange? He was completely besotted with Emerson, and it must have started from the very beginning. Something about her called to him in a way that no other woman ever had.

The sadness on her face was like a sucker punch to his gut. She didn't want him to sell the bar. The truth was he didn't know yet what he was going to do. He could only confirm that it was still a possibility. He had to try to explain that to her.

"It's just that I…" he began.

She took a breath, seemingly to center herself. "I know."

Did she? She couldn't possibly understand something that he didn't. "We've been so busy getting ready for this. We haven't had time to talk about my plans." He gestured with his arm to indicate the party.

"I only thought that once you saw how hard I worked—I mean, how great the bar turned out and all of the potential it had…"

"It's amazing and you worked magic here, beyond my expectations."

"Still, you've made up your mind. You're definitely going to sell the bar and move away?"

She bit her lip, and if he wasn't mistaken, she was holding her breath. Jack's heart soared at the idea of his presence affecting someone so much. When was the last time anyone had cared if he stayed or went?

Xander said something under his breath that sounded very much like, "Jack always leaves." But Jack ignored it. Instead he touched a hand to Emerson's shoulder.

"Hey, I haven't decided anything yet."

"But you're leaning more toward going." She lowered her voice. "Aren't you?"

"I…" he began. Only, he couldn't finish the sentence. If she had asked him this same question a few weeks earlier, his answer would have been a resounding yes. Now…he simply didn't know.

She was waiting, and her eyes were becoming huge blue saucers. He wished he could tell her what she wanted to hear. But he wouldn't lie to her.

He closed his mouth. She nodded and abruptly turned and walked away.

Damn. A different, harsher oath tore out from his lips.

"What's wrong with you?" Xander asked, oblivious.

He eyed his friend long and hard.

"What?" Xander asked.

"Did you have to say that? In front of her?"

"Say what?" Xander took a long swig of beer. His gaze followed Emerson as she crossed the room and met with Trina. The two exchanged some words. It looked like Trina tried to entice Emerson to the dance floor, but Emerson shook her head. "About you leaving?"

"Yes, that."

"So what?" Xander asked. "What's the big deal?" He stepped back and cocked his head. "Wait a minute." He pointed his finger at Jack and then in the general direction of Emerson and then back to Jack. "This thing between you is fake. Right? It's a pretend relationship."

Jack swallowed. Hard. "Of course. We're pretending for her parents, and she helped me spruce up the bar."

Again, Xander looked from him to Emerson and back again. His hands fell to his side as he squeezed his eyes shut. "Damn. I'm sorry, man. I didn't realize."

"Realize what?"

"That while you and Emerson were so busy pretending to like each other, you actually started to *like* each other."

Jack shuffled backward a few steps. "No, we didn't do that."

All Xander had to respond with was a raised eyebrow.

Jack slumped back into his chair. Xander followed, sitting in the chair next to him, which Emerson had abandoned.

"Yeah, okay, I like her. A lot."

"Dude, this became complicated."

"I don't think I've ever done complicated." He shrugged. "Never wanted to." *Until now. Until Emerson.*

What did that mean? Because, despite admitting his feelings, he still didn't know what to do about the bar. Was liking a woman enough to make him stay in one place? To stop flitting from location to location, trying to figure out where he wanted to be?

He didn't know the answers.

"I upset her just now."

Xander grimaced. "Actually, I think I did. I'm an idiot," he uttered softly.

"Well, we already knew that," Jack said with a grin. But his smile quickly faded. "I don't know what to say to her at this point."

"Do you want to stay here in Virginia?"

Jack ran a hand over his face. "I'm not sure."

"So you want to sell the bar and leave?"

He rubbed the back of his neck. "Not sure about that either."

Xander leaned back in his chair. "One thing is for sure. You need to erase that frown from her face." He jutted his chin toward Emerson, who was on her cell phone, at the other end of the bar.

His friend was right. Without saying so, Jack rose. He watched Emerson end the call and put her cell back into her pocket. Then he quickly crossed the room in eager strides.

"Em, listen, I want to say something."

She looked up, crossing her arms over her chest. Her body language spoke volumes. She was closing herself off to him.

"About before, what Xander said." He shook his head. "No, about what I said. The thing is, I'm a bit in limbo right now."

"You don't owe me any explanations, Jack."

"Yes, I do." How to explain to her when he couldn't make sense of it himself? "My dad's passing was extremely unexpected. I never imagined that one phone call would have me rushing back here and taking over a business that I'm not exactly qualified to run."

Something knowing sparkled in her eyes and she actually smiled.

"What?" he asked.

"I wish you could see yourself the way I've seen you the last couple of weeks."

Her words mirrored what he so often thought about her. He desperately wanted her to view herself the way he did, but never did he expect her to turn that sentiment back on him.

"You're a natural at this." She gestured around the bar.

He snorted. "Oh yeah. I didn't even know how much vodka to order."

She rolled her eyes. "Don't be ridiculous. You handled it. You handled every detail and decision in reopening this place. When you didn't know the answer, you asked the appropriate person. You made this night happen."

He shook his head vigorously. "No, you made this night happen."

She emitted a humorless laugh. "I planned a party. You ran a bar."

Well, huh. She held such conviction in her eyes that it actually stopped him in his tracks. Was she right? Was this true? He had to admit that he'd been enjoying himself where the bar was concerned. One of the best parts of his jobs out in Vegas and Reno was interacting with people. Just like the bar.

She was looking at him with such big, beautiful eyes. And those pouty, tempting lips. He couldn't resist. No man could.

Jack leaned toward her and pressed his lips to hers. The action elicited a small moan from her and Jack took the opportunity to draw her farther into his arms.

The kiss turned steamy fast, and he was sure that was his doing. Kissing Emerson had become as essential to him, in the last couple of weeks, as air.

All of the sounds of the bar—the music, the laughter, the clinking of glasses—simply faded away. Nothing mattered. Only Emerson and her succulent mouth.

"Come home with me," he mumbled against her mouth. A mouth that turned up into a lazy smile.

Her eyes opened. She ran her hands through the hair at the base of his neck. "You may have noticed that you have a bar full of people at the moment."

Oh. Right. "They won't notice."

"Jack," she said, exasperated. "This is a big night for you."

"And I would like to celebrate it with someone who is incredibly special to me."

She swallowed hard. "Me?"

He nipped her bottom lip. "You."

"Okay."

"Hey—will you come home with me?"

"At the end of the night. Yes. Now I have to get back to the party."

She began walking away, but he quickly reached for her hand and grabbed hold. She peeked over her shoulder.

"We're good, right?"

She hesitated, for a brief moment. "We're fine."

Only, there was something in her eyes. A certain shadow that led him to believe that fine was the opposite of what they were.

Because he was falling hard for Emerson Dewitt and he suspected his feelings were reciprocated. Which meant, Xander had been right. This had gotten complicated.

And if he wasn't careful, they were both in very real danger of getting hurt.

Chapter Eleven

Emerson was bone-tired.

Jack pulled his truck into the driveway, and they slowly made their way up the path and into the house through the front door. He turned on a small lamp on the console table next to the door.

Cosmo came barreling out of the living room, with his tail wagging at a hundred miles an hour.

"Cosmo," Emerson squealed and leaned down to pet and rub and fawn. "Hello, handsome boy."

Jack laughed.

"I wish you were more animated with my dog," he said sarcastically.

Emerson straightened. She stared at Jack until he questioned her.

"What?"

"You just referred to Cosmo as your dog. Not your dad's dog."

As if conveying his own excitement at this development, Cosmo jumped up on Jack, placing his two front paws on his thighs and attempting to lick his crotch. Jack laughed and pushed the dog down. Then he crouched and rubbed Cosmo's belly.

Jack coughed. "Well, the little guy has been growing on me."

Emerson grinned from ear to ear. Watching Jack with the dog was melting her heart. She sighed.

All of the adrenaline of the day was crashing around her, and she knew she could curl up right here on the floor of the foyer and sleep for twelve straight hours. Thank God tomorrow was Sunday and she didn't have any pressing events coming up. In fact, she could sleep all day, if she wanted. Probably, she would.

It was always like this after a big event. For some unknown reason, she actually thrived on the feeling.

Spending days, weeks or months planning every scenario, every angle of an event. When the execution day arrived, she lived on nerves and coffee, running from one to-do item to the next. She darted between crises, put out fires and made sure that no one was the wiser.

But a point always came when all of that energy faded. For the Mitchell-Cross party, that point had arrived. It was three o'clock in the morning and she'd been awake for almost twenty-four hours straight.

She stopped in the middle of the floor and let out a long, tired yawn.

"You must be beyond beat," Jack said. He came up behind her and removed her coat. Then he took her purse and the large tote bag she'd used and put them away.

"Come on." He urged her to a bench at the base of the stairs. Forcing her to sit, he knelt in front of her and removed her boots. One at a time.

The heels on her boots were miniscule, since she had

known that it would be a long day on her feet. Still, she wouldn't be surprised if her feet didn't let out a full-blown cheer as they were freed from the shoes.

"Give me one sec. I want to let Cosmo out back and make sure he has food and water. Don't go anywhere."

As if she could go somewhere, even if she wanted. That would involve moving, and she definitely didn't have the energy for that. Emerson leaned back and closed her eyes.

She wasn't sure how much time had passed, but she sensed Jack's presence again. "Where's Cosmo?"

"He went out back and did his business. Now he's having a nice late-night snack." He peered down at her. "Have I thanked you for everything you did yet?"

"You don't have to thank me. It's my job."

"I didn't pay you."

"I love doing it and, besides, you're paying me back. And the currency you're using is much more precious than dollar bills. After all, you still have to spend more time with Beatrice and Walter Dewitt. My parents' anniversary party is next Friday."

"It will be fine, Em."

She shook her head, too tired to elaborate on it. "I can't even think about that now."

Her eyes fluttered closed as the remaining energy left her body. But they flew open again when she was hoisted into the air. Jack had hooked one arm under her legs and the other behind her back. He carried her as if she weighed nothing.

"Jack," she said.

He pressed a soft kiss to her lips. "Shh. I got you."

He walked them up the stairs, down the hallway and into the bedroom he was using. Gently, he placed her on the bed.

The room was dark, and besides the sound of a light rain that had started falling while they drove home, the house was silent. It was so different out where Jack lived than it was where she lived, in Old Town. Even though Jack's house was a quick drive away, in the Del Ray neighborhood, sometimes it felt like they were far away in the country.

It was nice. Calming. Relaxing, even, to be away from the hustle of the heart of the city.

Jack didn't turn any lights on. She heard him removing his shoes, but she couldn't even lift her tired head from the pillow. The mattress shifted when he joined her.

She reached for him. Wanted to feel that he really was right next to her.

Tonight had brought a lot of unexpected emotions. She'd worked hard on this party. Put her whole self into making it perfect. She'd wanted it to be perfect for him. Wanted him to see the possibilities.

But there was that very real moment that had threatened to crush her heart. Jack's future was unknown. This was something that didn't come as a surprise, yet she'd been so busy falling for him that she'd allowed herself to forget about it and push it from her mind.

She needed to protect herself. There was a very real possibility of getting hurt again. Thinking about how much her breakup with Thad had affected her was one thing. With Jack, she already felt more for him than she had for her ex-fiancé. She didn't even want to imagine the pain of actually watching him walk away. So she definitely needed to guard her heart.

But at the moment, she was too tired to fight it. When Jack rolled over, propping himself so he could gaze down at her, she didn't move.

Usually the passion was so explosive between them.

When he leaned over and softly pressed a kiss to one of her eyelids, then the other, then the tip of her nose, and finally to her lips, she realized tonight was going to be different.

He kissed her for a long time, moving his lips warmly and gently over hers. She reached up to cup the back of his head. He deepened the kiss and she sighed, welcoming him in.

Moving his lips to her jawline, he showered her with soft, gentle kisses. He ran his lips down her neck, stopping only to nip her earlobe.

His every movement was relaxing her beyond anything she'd ever felt before. Her limbs were starting to feel heavy, even as her heartbeat began racing.

Jack was running his lips, his tongue, his teeth, along her collarbone and following the neckline of her blouse. When she made to move, Jack reared back and shook his head.

"No?" she asked, surprised.

"Tonight is all about you. It's for you."

Her heart soared. His face was so serious and his eyes full of hazy lust. Maybe this really could be something. Whatever this thing was between them. This thing that had begun as a bargain to help each other out. This thing that had clearly taken on a life of its own.

She'd done her very best to live up to what she thought he wanted tonight, at the bar. And now he was rewarding her. Did that mean he'd stay in town?

Because if their relationship really only was a bargain, half of it was over. After her parents' anniversary party, they wouldn't have any reason to stay together.

Then Jack was removing her blouse, and any deep thinking ceased. With her shirt off and thrown to the floor, he ran his hands up and down her sides. A small giggle escaped her lips when he brushed over her ticklish spot. He grinned before leaning down and licking that very spot. Emerson sucked in a breath.

His clever mouth was warming every inch of her body. She wasn't even self-conscious about her bra. She always wore a more-supportive and less-sexy bra when she was working. But Jack didn't seem to notice or care. He simply unhooked it and immediately covered one nipple with his warm mouth and sucked gently. She reached for him and held him tightly.

He was showering her with attention and, dare she think it, love? Not one area of her body was neglected as he pulled her pants and black satin panties down her legs. His hands, his mouth and his tongue explored every bit of her.

When he moved to the end of the bed and reached for her foot, she opened her eyes and realized he was still fully clothed, while she was naked and bare before him. Normally she would feel self-conscious, but she didn't with Jack. It was as simple as that. When she was with him, she was completely and irrevocably herself.

He sucked her big toe into his mouth and she squirmed. "Jack, my feet are horrible." She desperately needed a pedicure, and her feet were completely gross after the long winter. Not to mention standing on them all day long.

He tilted his head and studied her. "Your feet are beautiful, just like the rest of your body."

To prove it, he dragged a lazy hand up from her foot, over her calf and thigh, her stomach, her breasts, until he reached her head. He cupped it as he lay on top of her. Then he kissed her so deeply and so very passionately. She was being pulled under big-time, and she was sure she'd never be able to find her way back up to the surface again.

That might just be okay. Did she really need to return to reality when it felt this good to be with him?

Finally, he ended the kiss and stood. Seemingly in no hurry, he took her in. His eyes traveled over every inch of her, from her aching toes to the top of her head. Then back down again. A slow, sexy smile spread across his face.

"What's that for?"

"You have no idea what it's doing to me to see you like that."

She snorted. "What? Lying here like a big old lump?"

He licked his lips and his eyes narrowed in on her. It was as if he were the hungriest man on the planet and she was a big, juicy steak. He looked like he was about to salivate.

"You haven't had your fill yet?" she asked.

"Sweetheart, with you, I don't think I'll ever have enough."

Her heart flipped over. She gulped.

"Then why don't you get over here and start making a dent in that appetite."

He grinned. Then he shed his clothes and opened the drawer of the nightstand on the side of the bed. She knew that's where he kept his protection.

After he returned to her, he hovered over her, stroking her cheek with one of his fingers. Then he kissed her again, slowly, deeply. His hands roamed over her skin again, caressing her breasts, teasing her, setting her insides on fire. But he never stopped kissing her.

"Jack," she murmured against his lips.

"Mmm?"

She nipped at his bottom lip. "I want you."

He pushed a strand of hair back from her face. "Now?"

"Please."

He framed her face in his hands and kissed her one

more time. Then he pushed inside her. They both moaned. The pleasure was absolutely exquisite.

They moved together, completely in concert. They'd been together enough times now for their bodies to understand each other.

Jack reached for her hands and brought them to the pillow, next to her ears. They clasped fingers. Their eyes locked on to each other.

They were joined in every way possible. Their bodies, their eyes, their hands. Their hearts?

It was the most sensual moment of her life. She held on tightly as Jack's movements became faster and harder. As she went right over the edge, with him following right behind.

And then they collapsed into each other, completely sated, as the rain continued to fall.

The rain had picked up. It was drumming a fast *tat, tat, tat* against the roof of the house. The wind was roaring through the trees, and a loose branch was scratching the window.

She and Jack were lying in bed, tangled up in the sheets and each other's limbs as they listened to the sounds of the storm. Cosmo had found his way upstairs and made himself at home at the bottom of the bed. He was curled up in a little ball, seemingly fast asleep. But every once in a while, he would perk up, lick one of their toes and then return to his slumber.

Emerson still felt exhausted, only she now also felt rejuvenated, energized, sated. It was a strange sensation.

"Two weeks ago, we did this for the first time," Jack said.

It was a rare moment of reflection for him. She ran a hand over his bare chest.

"I made love to you under the stars. I felt bad that we were on the hard, cold ground."

"I liked being outside." She had. She remembered thinking that they couldn't possibly do *that* outside. But then they had, and she'd felt empowered. She'd also felt sexy as hell.

"We could go in the backyard now, if you want," he said with a wry smile.

"Nah. It's raining."

"I thought rain was romantic."

"It is. But it can be from inside, as well." She shifted her body against a certain part of his as a reminder of just how sexy rain could be.

He grinned and nuzzled her neck. "Are you okay? Do you need anything?"

"Funny, but I am feeling quite reenergized. Although, some water would be great." She made to move but he stopped her by pushing her back against the pillows. He tucked the blankets around her and kissed her forehead.

"I got it. Be right back."

She watched him rise, in all of his naked glory. She would never tire of looking at this man's naked body. Sadly, he pulled on his boxer briefs before leaving the room.

Cosmo let out a little harrumph at the disturbance. Then he made his way up the bed and made himself comfortable in a ball on Jack's pillow. Emerson laughed and ran a hand over his soft fur.

Jack returned a few minutes later with two glasses of water. She sat up in bed and drank almost the entire glass. Cosmo lifted his head with mild interest and took in the scene. Then he rose, circled around a couple of times before returning to his cute little ball position.

"Seriously, dog? On my pillow?"

"I think it's a sign of love," Emerson suggested with a laugh.

"When you're not here, he lays on your pillow."

Her pillow. How domestic. A little thrill ran through her.

Jack climbed back into bed and sat up against a mound of pillows. He gathered Cosmo up and nestled him on his stomach. She placed her glass on the nightstand and curled up next to him, laying her head on his chest. His fingers ran lazy circles over her back, and her eyes began to close.

Suddenly, Jack said, "I think my dad would have liked the party tonight."

Her eyes flew open. She wasn't sure how to respond. Luckily, she didn't have to.

"He really liked when the bar was full. He enjoyed people having fun, laughing, relaxing. The more bodies that crammed into The Wright Drink, the bigger his smile got."

"Then I'm sure he would have been entertained by tonight. All that dancing and karaoke."

He chuckled. "I'll never hear 'Baby Got Back' quite the same way again."

Emerson bit her lip as she contemplated asking him a question. But it was something that she'd been wondering about since she had met him. "Jack, can I ask you something?"

"Of course."

"The way you talk about your dad… Did you not get along?" She twisted her head so she could see his face, his reaction.

He shrugged and readjusted, sitting back against the headboard. "We did. But he got along with the bar more."

"Must have been tough on both of you," she said, more

to herself than him. "By nature, a bar is open on week-ends and at night. That must have been hard on him."

"Before my mom passed away, we would actually go have dinner at the bar most nights. This guy, Larry, was the cook then. He would always make sure to have kid-friendly options for me. Grilled cheese sandwiches, chicken nuggets—that kind of stuff."

He was relaxing. He was opening up. Emerson wanted to punch a fist in the air in triumph, but she also wanted to hear his memories. Understand him better. So she didn't move, except to pet the dog. Only listened.

"My mom insisted I get vegetables too. So Larry would always include carrots or asparagus." He rolled his eyes but was still smiling. "There was always a salad waiting for my mom. My dad used to say that she was half rabbit because she ate so much salad.

"Dad bought the pinball machine, the *Pac-Man* game and the air-hockey table for me. Someone was always willing to take me on. Thought they could win over a kid." His eyes were practically sparkling with what were clearly happy memories. "But I was good."

"Oh really?"

"Well, I was there every day. I was a little swindler really."

"Sounds like a fun way to grow up."

"It was. At least it was interesting."

She reached for his hand and was happy when he let her take it. He began running his thumb over her skin, and the small gesture sent shockwaves through her body.

"I can't tell you how many times my mom would end up behind the bar, helping out. Then someone would play a slow song on the jukebox. My dad would scoop her up in his arms and they would dance together."

"That sounds so sweet."

He nodded. "Even the people waiting for their drinks or food didn't seem to mind. They would just watch my parents dance together behind the bar."

His fingers tightened around hers.

"Then one day I came home from school, and both of my parents were waiting for me in the living room. My mom had been to the doctor. She had an aggressive form of cancer."

Emerson swallowed a large gulp on a very dry throat.

"She died only two months later."

She wanted to say something. Anything that would bring him some comfort. But what could you say to someone who lost a parent at such an impressionable age?

"After that, my dad was always at the bar. The house was empty, cold. Lonely. Things changed."

Emerson stifled a sigh. It sounded like his dad had probably spent the same amount of time at the bar after his mother's death as he had before. Only, without his mother around, his perspective shifted and everything felt different.

"I stopped dropping by the bar," Jack continued. "At first, I had no way to get there. I couldn't drive yet," he explained. "Then I was pretty active in high school. Baseball, girls…" He offered a grin, but it didn't quite reach his eyes.

"I wanted to talk to my dad about my mom. I missed her," he said softly.

Emerson shifted slightly. "He didn't talk about her?"

Jack shook his head. "Never. To be honest, he barely spoke to me about anything after her death. He would make sure I had done my homework. He would always ask if I ate. Tell me to clean up my room. The essential stuff. But we never had a long conversation again. Even later in life, speaking over the phone was like pulling teeth."

No wonder he hadn't wanted to return home.

"I wanted to talk about her," he repeated.

Emerson's heart clenched at the raw desperation in his voice.

"Needed to talk about her. I would come home from school to an empty house. My dad was already at the bar. Her perfume lingered in the house. Her clothes were in the laundry room for I don't know how long. And I just wanted to talk about her and remember everything."

Emerson gulped. "Did your mom work?"

"Yeah, she was a teacher in the local elementary school."

His dad had to make up for an extra income. They went from being a two-income household to one.

So, there was a father and son, both grieving the loss of a very special woman, while they went on with life. Lives that would never be the same again.

A realization struck Emerson at that point. Jack wasn't considering leaving Virginia because of his father. He was running away from his mother. From her memory and from the pain that memory brought forth.

She closed her eyes as the thought washed over her. Jack was still grieving for the mom he'd lost way too young. He'd probably never really allowed himself to say goodbye. Because his dad had seemed to shut down after his wife's death, Jack had never gotten the closure he needed. That's why he ran from place to place. That's the reason he didn't settle somewhere and put down roots.

That was probably why he wouldn't stay now.

She wanted him to stay because she loved him. But he was going to leave because he couldn't bring himself to stay in a place where the memory of his mother would haunt him.

How could she ever ask him to?

Chapter Twelve

Even though they were right on time for her parents' anniversary party, Emerson and Jack had to circle the block a couple of times before they found a parking space. It seemed like everyone in Northern Virginia had come out to help the Dewitts celebrate.

Thirty years of marriage.

Despite any hard feelings with her mother, she couldn't help but be happy for them. Getting to the pearl anniversary was no easy feat.

Sometimes it seemed like Beatrice and Walter were so very different. Her dad was so much more laid-back than her mom. He would be content to live in a one-bedroom cabin on a lake, fishing, reading mystery novels and watching World War II documentaries, while her mom delighted in things like flower arrangements, china patterns and hosting tea parties.

Yet they were one unit. A strongly bonded couple that

had raised two daughters, while starting their own businesses.

"What are you thinking?"

She glanced at Jack as they walked from their parking space at the end of the street. He looked so handsome tonight in a black suit and silver tie. He'd left his stubble though, and the contrast with the suit was absolutely mouthwatering.

"About my parents."

"Thirty years is amazing," he replied. "You know what else is amazing?"

She stopped and waited for his reply.

"You in that dress."

She felt a grin spread across her face.

Her mother had strongly suggested she wear a tasteful black dress to the event tonight. Being the good daughter she was, Emerson had complied. But with Jack's idea to make it her own. She was wearing a midi-length black dress with a conservative neckline that was classic and sophisticated. From the front. When she turned around, the big reveal was a low cut back. For an extra splash of whimsy, she'd pinned a bejeweled turquoise flower in her curls.

Tasteful black, without losing herself.

"I feel good." She didn't know where the statement came from. But it was true. She did feel good. Strong. Like herself. When was the last time she could claim that?

Tonight, she felt strong and confident. Even though her mother was sure to dislike her outfit choice, and everyone inside the party would no doubt fawn all over her sister, Emerson didn't care.

She had a growing business that she'd started all on her own. She adored her friends. Over the last couple of weeks, she'd had a strong, handsome, fun, interesting man by her side. It may have started off as a pretend relationship, but she knew that was no longer the case. Her feelings wouldn't lie. Her heart couldn't lie. And the way Jack held her in his arms definitely wasn't a lie.

Jack stepped toward her. He had that look on his face she'd come to know so well. His eyes darkened and he was about to kiss her. She held her breath in anticipation.

His lips brushed over hers, once, twice, before delving into a much deeper, passionate kiss. Right there, in the middle of the street, as cars whizzed by, searching for parking spaces, and guests walked toward her parents' house.

She could care less that they were in the middle of a crowd. Her hands came up to frame his face. To keep him anchored to her as she took and took.

When they broke apart, he ran a finger over her cheek so lightly. It was a move that he did with her more and more often. Her stomach flipped. The lightest touch from him seemed to set her soul on fire.

No words passed between them. Rather, he reached for her hand, interlacing their fingers as they continued toward the house.

"Looks great," Jack commented with a head tilt.

Emerson had to agree. The outside of her parents' house looked even more perfect than usual. And that was saying something. The whole place was glowing. She wouldn't put it past her mother to have hired someone to power wash each and every brick. The glass in the windows was sparkling, the beige trim impeccable.

Wreaths hung from the windows. Lights were on inside, which illuminated the outline of people talking and laughing. For such a large house, there was a homey quality.

The front yard had been spruced up after the winter.

New flowers had been planted and surrounded by mulch. The driveway and sidewalk glimmered, thanks to a rainstorm that happened the night before.

Along with two couples she recognized from her dad's law firm, they entered the house. Music was playing softly through the hidden speakers her parents had installed throughout the house. Yummy aromas wafted from room to room. She knew her mother had hired her favorite caterer and servers were passing all kinds of different appetizers. The furniture had been rearranged to make cozy sitting corners and places to invite conversations.

They made their way through the crowd. When they passed the patio doors, she could see that her mother had made sure the outside was also party-ready. Lanterns and twinkly lights illuminated the patio. Heat lamps lined the perimeter, and a bar was set up on one side.

"Your parents sure do have a lot of friends," Jack said.

He seemed to be surveying the space as they searched for her parents.

"Daddy started his own firm decades ago. Between colleagues and clients, he knows a lot of people. And Mama…" She whistled. "I can't even begin to describe the amount of people in her life."

Jack jutted his chin toward the left. "There's Charlie." He waved. "Hey, buddy."

Despite having spent hours together at dinner, Charlie seemed temporarily confused as to who Jack was. He took in Emerson and his jaw worked back and forth.

"Hi, Emerson. Hi…" His phone went off. Immediately, he put it to his ear and walked away.

"Always good chatting with you," Jack called to his retreating back.

Emerson laughed.

"God, I love that man," Jack said, and had her laughter turn into a snort.

"I don't know where my parents are."

"Let's get a drink to fortify the search efforts," he said, smiling at her.

They found another bar in the dining room and got two whiskeys, neat. Sipping their drinks, they stood against the wall. Emerson waved to the occasional person and exchanged greetings with some of her mother's friends.

Everyone she chatted with seemed quite taken with Jack. She knew that, in the looks department, he was quite different from the men she'd dated in the past. With his stubble, dark looks and mischievous grin, Jack was attracting a lot of attention. In fact, people—particularly the female guests—were so charmed by him that they didn't even harp on the fact that Emerson had a new boyfriend as she'd expected.

Amelia entered the room, wearing a navy wrap dress with a gorgeous diamond necklace. Emerson knew the necklace had been a wedding present from their parents. Her hair was off her face, highlighting her long neck. Emerson peered at her sister. Her makeup looked fabulous, as always, but she knew Mia. Emerson worried her lip.

"What's wrong?" Jack asked.

"I'm not sure. Something seems off with my sister."

Jack's gaze sought out Amelia. He studied her before returning his attention to Emerson. "Everyone seems excited to see her."

The room did come alive when Amelia entered, as if a spotlight shone directly on her. Conversations stopped and everyone wanted a turn to say hi.

The feeling Emerson had didn't subside though. In fact, as she watched her sister interacting with the party-goers, it only increased.

Amelia, you look amazing. As always.

How's married life treating you?

Still working at your mom's shop? Well, as soon as you start having babies, you won't have to do that anymore.

Where's that handsome husband of yours?

With each question, Amelia appeared to withdraw more into herself. Her face continued to fall, and as she neared their side of the room, Emerson could actually see dark circles under her eyes. Of course, Amelia had expertly covered them with makeup, but she knew her sister like the back of her hand.

Finally, Amelia reached her and Jack.

"Hey, Mia. Love your dress. When did you get that?"

Amelia looked down at the dress as if she had forgotten she was even wearing it. "Oh. I think I got it when I went with Charlie on one of his business trips. I needed something to do."

What a weird comment. Emerson opened her mouth, but Jack beat her to it. He drew Amelia into a big hug, which actually seemed to calm her. When they pulled back, she asked about the bachelor/bachelorette party. They exchanged words, and then Amelia pointed at Emerson's glass.

"What are you drinking?"

She reached for the glass and had it to her lips so fast that Emerson almost didn't get out, "Wait, it's scotch." But Amelia took a long drink.

"I need some of this."

"You don't like scotch," Emerson pointed out.

"Would you like me to get you something?" Jack asked.

"Get her a glass of wine. Rosé," Emerson said.

Once Jack was out of earshot, she turned to her sister. "What is up with you tonight?"

Amelia shrugged.

Emerson held her ground. She crossed her arms over her chest and waited.

Amelia sighed. "I thought everyone would be over asking me about being married. You're the one with the new boyfriend. They should be peppering you with intrusive questions."

"They're all too gaga over Jack's hotness to care about me." Emerson giggled but noticed that her sister remained stoic.

"Your wedding was only six months ago. Sorry, sis, you're still a hot topic." She tugged on Mia's hair, something she used to do when they were little. "What's the problem anyway? Since when do you shy away from attention?"

"Since I feel...embarrassed about my answers."

What? "Embarrassed? What in the world do you have to be embarrassed about?"

Amelia opened her mouth, about to answer, but Jack returned with her glass of wine. She downed half a glass in one gulp. She looked directly at Emerson. But Emerson got the distinct feeling that she wasn't really seeing her.

"Where's Grace? I thought she was coming tonight," she asked distractedly.

"Where else?" Emerson said. "It's Saturday. She had a wedding. But she'll be by later."

Amelia nodded. "I need to find Charlie," she said abruptly.

Jack watched her walk away. "Is she okay?"

"I'm honestly not sure."

"Emerson, Jack." Beatrice's voice echoed across the room.

Emerson took in her mother, wearing a gorgeous cranberry-colored dress with silver heels. Her dad looked handsome in one of his crisp black suits. They made such a picturesque couple. Her dad paused to press a kiss to his wife's forehead. Despite everything, her parents truly loved each other.

"It's go time," Jack whispered in her ear.

"You look beautiful, Mama."

Beatrice ran a hand over Emerson's hair, pausing on her jeweled clip. "I see you wore black."

"As you suggested."

She coughed lightly. "You look lovely."

Emerson's mouth fell open. Had her mother just complimented her? And about her clothes? When was the last time that happened? Had it ever happened?

Jack jumped in. "She does look great, doesn't she."

Emerson finally recovered. "It doesn't matter what I'm wearing. Everyone is here to see you."

She surprised both herself and her mother when she pulled her in for a tight hug. Then she whispered in her ear, "You look absolutely stunning, Mama. As usual."

Pulling back, Beatrice studied her carefully, with a small tilt of the head. "Something is different about you tonight, Emerson."

Emerson twirled around.

"Seriously, Emerson Rose?" her mother said.

She actually giggled. She'd forgotten about the low back of her dress.

"There are elderly people here tonight."

That just made Emerson laugh more.

Beatrice tapped a French-manicured finger against her lips. "Still, something is different. You seem..."

"Happy?" Emerson couldn't keep the smile from blossoming.

Her mother's gaze scooted over to Jack, who was listening to one of her dad's joke, and then back to her. "In love," her mother said firmly, knowingly, in that way only mothers had.

She had two options. She could deny it, or she could own it. Maybe it was being at her parents' thirtieth wedding anniversary. Maybe it was the fact that every time she looked over at Jack, she got a certain tingle in her stomach. Or maybe it was because she was sick of lying about something that was no longer a lie.

In any case, it was finally time for a little truth.

She met her mother's stare head-on.

"Yes, I am."

Jack was enjoying himself. Maybe a little too much.

He'd been talking and laughing with Emerson's father for the last fifteen minutes. Emerson was deep in conversation with her mother, except for when another guest would interrupt them to offer congratulations and well wishes.

He was introduced to person after person as Emerson's new boyfriend. Mr. Dewitt bragged about Jack's bar, telling colleagues and friends that they had to stop by next time they were in Old Town.

Even Mrs. Dewitt had seemed to come around to the fact that he owned a bar. She was boasting about her painting job in The Wright Drink. She actually winked at him as one of her friends asked him questions about owning a bar.

Jack was feeling like a part of the family.

He grabbed another drink and took a moment to get some fresh air. He stepped outside, onto the patio, and found a quiet corner.

Part of the Dewitt family. Part of Emerson's life. He wasn't sure how to take that idea, because his head was telling him it was a dangerous place to go. But his heart really liked the thought of having people to support him. Of being part of a family again. Of being there to support the woman in his life, every day.

It felt good to be part of such a momentous event. Thirty years of marriage. He couldn't help but think about his parents. No doubt if his mom had survived the cancer, they would have stayed together. They had adored each other.

It was little things with his parents. Small shows of affection. His mom always brought his dad coffee in bed, fixed just the way he liked it. His dad left little notes for his mom around the house. He brought her flowers all the time too. Daisies.

The same flowers he'd given to Emerson when they had gone out on their first date.

Wow. He hadn't even realized. It was like his father's gesture had seeped into his subconscious.

His parents were a unit. They were home for each other.

Jack had been all over the world. Experienced everything, from jumping out of a plane in Hungary to seeing the Leaning Tower of Pisa to hiking a volcano in Hawaii. Yet he'd mostly been alone on those adventures.

Mr. Dewitt seemed interested in his stories. It was nice to have someone to share them with. He'd told a couple to Emerson and had enjoyed watching her eyes widen as he had detailed walking along the Great Wall of China and snorkeling along the Barrier Reef.

He was starting to realize that it would have been nice to have these same conversations with his dad, whom he'd basically denied a relationship with.

"Someone is deep in thought."

Clearly he had been, since he hadn't even heard Xander creep up on him.

"What are you doing here?" he asked as Xander squeezed a lime into a gin and tonic before taking a sip.

"My firm does a lot of work with Mr. Dewitt's. I've actually known your pretend girlfriend's dad for a couple of years now. Speaking of your pretend girlfriend, where is she?"

Jack pushed a hand through his hair. "Actually, I wouldn't say we're all that pretend anymore."

"Nooo." Xander overexaggerated the word and put a hand to his chest like he was in shock.

Jack answered by way of a finger of choice in Xander's direction. For his part, Xander simply chuckled.

"Give me all the fingers you want. But the truth is the truth."

Jack loosened his tie. "And what exactly is the truth here?"

"That you've fallen hard for Emerson and it's been clear to anyone with half an eye that the two of you are wild for each other."

"Interesting, since I didn't even know that."

"Well, you've always been on the slow side."

Jack punched him in the arm, and Xander feigned being hurt.

"So, you think this thing with Emerson is a good thing?"

Xander's jovial expression slowly faded. He studied the contents of his glass and swirled it around before finally talking. "You know me, dude. I can't get on board with any relationship."

"Why is that again?"

"It's what I believe. They don't work. They're not right. I see the results every day, in my work." He paused, glancing up. "But I do like seeing you happy, and if Emerson makes you happy, then great. As it turns out, I have something else that is going to make you happy."

Intrigued, Jack waited.

"I was finishing up some business with one of my clients today when he mentioned that he was looking to open a restaurant and bar. Asked if I knew of any locations."

For some reason, the hair on the back of Jack's neck stood up on high alert.

"I told the guy all about The Wright Drink. He was really into the location. Wants to know if he can come see it this week."

What should have been a happy development had the result of making Jack's stomach sink. Wasn't this what he wanted?

He took a long, deep breath.

"What?" Xander asked. "I thought this is what you wanted."

"It's definitely one possibility. I'm just not... I don't know."

Xander nodded knowingly, just as Emerson sidled up to them.

"There you are," she said.

He instinctively put his arm around her. She just felt so right up against his side.

"Needed some air," he said.

She laughed lightly. "Are you calling my parents' friends stuffy?"

"Oh no," Xander joined in. "They're all great. Barrels of fun."

"Shut up. When you two are my parents' age, you'll be having the same kinds of parties, talking to the same kinds of people."

Xander responded to that with a joke, but Jack didn't

really pay attention. He was too busy thinking about what Emerson had just said.

Would he and Xander still be friends in thirty years? Would they even be in the same place? If he sold the bar and left town, would they stay in touch? They had last time, but they were getting older.

"Jack."

He shook his head as Emerson pinned him with a look. "Sorry, what?"

"I asked what you guys were talking about before I walked up."

Jack looked to Xander, but his friend's lips were sealed shut. He'd clearly learned his lesson after the party in the bar.

But Jack didn't want to lie to Emerson.

"Xander has found a possible buyer for The Wright Drink."

He could feel the tension ratchet up between him and Emerson, as if someone were building a wall right between them.

He reached down and grabbed her hand, interlocking their fingers. He leaned over and whispered in her ear. "I haven't made any decisions yet."

"But you'll need to soon."

Unclear of how to respond, he simply nodded.

He didn't like the lines forming on her forehead or the way her lips were turned down in a frown. He wanted to tell her he would stay. But Jack just couldn't do that. Something was holding him back.

"Emerson—" But he was cut off as the patio doors opened and scores of party guests spilled out into the crisp night air.

"I think my parents are going to give a toast."

The interruption was probably better. He truly wasn't sure what he had been about to say back there.

People gathered in every available inch of space. Luckily, the Dewitt's had a spacious backyard and patio area.

Mr. and Mrs. Dewitt were the last people to step outside. They took up a spot under one of the porch lights, as if a spotlight were shining right on them. A microphone appeared from somewhere. Obviously this was not the first large party that had happened here.

They thanked everyone for being there. Then Mr. Dewitt kissed his wife's hand, and she handed him the microphone.

"Thirty years," he said as he turned his gaze on to his wife. The crowd broke out into applause and whistles.

"Thirty wonderful years," he amended, making Mrs. Dewitt laugh.

"What's the secret?" someone called out from the crowd.

Mr. Dewitt appeared thoughtful. "Well, I'll tell you what the secret is not. Perfection. People enter marriage thinking that their life will be perfect now that they've met their spouse."

Out of the corner of his eye, Jack noticed Amelia's husband, Charlie, walk away, leaving Amelia standing all alone, in the shadows beyond the patio. Emerson gestured for her sister to come stand by her and Jack, but Amelia shook her head.

"The thing is," Mr. Dewitt continued, "marriage is not a perfect union. There are often more hard times than good. Those are the times that define you.

"When Beatrice and I first married, I was offered an amazing new job. It was everything I had worked for, everything I wanted."

"But it was up here in Alexandria," Mrs. Dewitt chimed in.

"And that was scary for two people who had spent their lives in Spartanburg, South Carolina. But she followed me up here. Left her friends and family and everything she knew and made the move."

Once again, Mrs. Dewitt took the microphone. "I didn't understand the need to move to Northern Virginia, but I supported him anyway. Just like I dare say Walt didn't understand my need to open a wedding-dress boutique." Laughter spread throughout the crowd. "But he supported me every step of the way."

They leaned together for a quick kiss. The crowd clapped and cheered.

"I must be remiss to point out that it's not just about supporting the one you love. Equally essential is to be selfish from time to time. Be kind to yourself."

The speech went on and he heard plenty of "oohs" and "aahs" from the guests. But Jack had stopped listening. He was too concerned with the auburn-haired beauty next to him.

The one who had stopped holding his hand.

Chapter Thirteen

Emerson couldn't explain what had just happened.

All she knew was that she'd been listening to her parents' speech and something inside her had shifted. It felt like a weight she'd been carrying around for most of her life had been lifted.

Suddenly, she realized she was good enough. And not only because she was with Jack. She was enough on her own.

Her mother had spoken of being selfish and kind to yourself. Those words made something click in her mind.

She did support Jack. She understood his issues and the decision he had to make with his father's bar. She got—maybe more than he did himself—his hang-ups with his mother.

But dammit, where did *she* factor into the equation? It seemed like she was giving a lot more than he was.

Emerson didn't want to compete with a bar. Nor did

she want to be completely dismissed because of issues that Jack hadn't yet dealt with.

She was good enough and she wanted to be recognized. She wanted more than what she had right now.

As her parents' guests cheered and offered their congratulations, she backed away. Jack faced her.

"Em?" he asked, with curiosity and confusion in that one word.

Without warning, words exploded out of her mouth. "Are you going to stay here?"

Jack's eyes darkened, a contrast to the pallor his face had just taken on. She knew it was a ridiculous question. He'd just told her minutes ago that he hadn't made any decisions. But dammit, that was the point. Why was this so hard for him?

He reached for her hand, the hand she'd removed from his moments before. She took another step back.

His jaw was working, as if he wanted to say something. The problem was that she wasn't sure she wanted to hear it. So she turned and walked away, heading through the garden, away from the crowd.

She knew he was following her. Could feel his presence as she ended up at the same gazebo where they'd shared their first kiss.

"We're back here," he said, obviously referring to the gazebo.

"We've never left," she replied, speaking of something entirely different.

"What's going on, Em?"

She knew she needed to be straight with him. He deserved that. And she deserved some answers, as well. Even if the thought of him leaving town left her with a cold feeling in the pit of her stomach.

What she knew of Jack was that he didn't stay in one

place for long. Even though she'd realized a while ago that his wanderlust probably had to do with the loss of his mother, it didn't help her feel any more settled.

They'd started off as strangers who had made a deal to help each other, and then their fake relationship had evolved. For her, it wasn't pretend anymore. It hadn't been for quite some time. She didn't know when the change had occurred. Didn't really care.

Emerson realized that she felt more for Jack than she had for any other man in her life, including her former fiancé. How could that happen in such a short period of time?

All of those words her parents had spoken during their toast were real. They were true. They were the way she felt about Jack.

When he entered a room, her heart rate increased. When he wasn't around, her thoughts drifted to him. When he touched her, kissed her, made love to her, she thought of nothing else.

But that needed to change. It was time to start thinking of herself.

She leveled a serious stare at him. "Jack, I need to know if you're going to stick around. I deserve to know."

"Emerson," he began, throwing his palms up in front of him.

She shook her head. "No, don't do that. Don't evade the question." She took a long, deep breath. "We're not having a fake relationship anymore."

Silence hung between them. She could hear the other party guests talking and laughing near the house.

Finally, he said, "No, we're not."

She gestured back and forth between them. "This is real between us."

"Yes."

"Then you need to tell me your plans."

"Emerson, I don't know yet. I've been honest about that."

"I'm not saying you haven't been honest."

"Then, what are you saying?"

She fought the urge to rub her temples. A headache had begun to form. "I'm saying that if this is a real relationship between us, then I should be a part of your decision. I'm saying that, well, I'm worthy of a little respect."

He cocked his head. "Worthy? Of course you're worthy. You deserve respect and admiration. And...love."

"So why aren't you giving me any?"

It was the most empowering statement she'd ever made. She wished she'd said it earlier in her life. To her mother, her sister, her ex-fiancé. Instead she was saying it to the one person who had made her realize she could say it at all.

She wanted Jack. More than she could even believe. There was so much she would be willing to give up for him.

There was just one thing she valued higher than him. One thing she absolutely could not do without.

Herself.

Jack was flummoxed. Even though there was space— too much space—between them, he felt like she'd just reached into his chest and squeezed his heart until he couldn't breathe.

Emerson didn't think he was respecting her. Even though he tended to keep women and relationships in his life at arm's length, he'd always shown kindness and respect to any female in his life.

Still, she had a point. He'd been stringing her along because he couldn't make a decision. If he wasn't so hurt over her accusation, he would be proud of her. She was finally standing up for herself. Much to his detriment.

"Emerson, I never meant to—"

She quickly cut him off. "Even if you want to leave Alexandria because you don't want to own a bar or, hell, there's just some place you'd rather live, you are keeping me in the dark. If we're in a real relationship, you should be consulting me. Did it ever occur to you that I might want to come with you?"

He felt his mouth drop open. She would want to leave her life, her family and her business to go with him?

His earlier longing to be part of a family unit returned. How different his life would have been if Emerson had been by his side: traveling the world, experiencing all of the different adventures he'd had.

She was shaking her head, with disappointment written all over her face. "No, it hasn't occurred to you to talk to me about any of this. I guess you also haven't realized just how much I care about you. Or maybe the problem is that you don't care that much about me."

Now he did step toward her. He grabbed her upper arms and shook her lightly. "How in the hell can you say that?"

But he knew. It wasn't like he'd told her.

He released her arms and took her hands gently in his. Looking deep into her beautiful blue eyes, he said, "I care so much about you, Em. You've come to mean so much to me."

"Not enough."

He dropped her hands. She'd realized her power over him, and now she was running with it. He found himself growing irritated.

"I don't see what my feelings for you have to do with

my decision. It's mine to make. The consequences will be something I have to deal with. We only met a month ago."

Her eyes widened. For a second, he thought she might tear up. But she didn't. Instead she started to turn away, and that small action had his blood shooting to boil. He grabbed her arm and spun her back around to face him.

"What are you doing—?"

"No," he said, cutting her off. "What are *you* doing? Running away? Again."

"What is that supposed to mean?"

"It's what you do, isn't it? Things get heated and you climb out of a window."

Her mouth fell open and then quickly shut. He'd hit way below the belt and he knew it. The hurt in her eyes was the equivalent of a sucker punch to his gut.

"That's so not fair. That was one, and only one, time. Besides, it's laughable coming from you. You're the undisputed king of running when things get tough."

A truer statement had never been uttered. She knew it was true, and she knew that he knew it was true. Still, he couldn't admit that. Not to her. Not to anyone.

"When was the last time you were in town, Jack? How long did you stay away from Alexandria?" She shoved a hand through her hair, dislodging the pretty sparkly flower she'd anchored in her curls.

"You know I have regrets about that," he said.

"And yet you kept running. What happened when things didn't go right on a job? You'd run. You ran and ran and ran."

"Emerson, damn it. At least I did things for myself. At least I wasn't afraid to go after what I wanted, no matter what anyone thought. I never cared if I was disappointing my family. I did things for me."

She jutted a stubborn chin out. "And look where that got you. All alone."

"Better than being overly dependent on my mother's opinions of me."

She let out a sound of annoyance. "You know what? I don't need this kind of BS right now. Especially not from you."

She was right. She already got enough grief from her mother. And she'd been through a really tough year.

He relented. "Your mother loves you, even if she stresses you out by being so…overprotective, shall we say? You know that you are amazing. Tonight, you stuck up for yourself with me. But now it's time for you to stand up to your mother."

Silence descended on them. It was as if the party had ceased. Even the creatures of the night stopped making their natural sounds. It was as if the whole universe had been shocked by his words. Jack knew the feeling. He held his breath, waiting on Emerson's reply to his request.

Tentatively, he glanced at Emerson. Her face expressed a dozen different emotions—most noticeably surprise— in a very short span of time.

"I'm sorry," they both said at the same time.

It was his turn to shove a hand through his hair. "What are you sorry for?"

She shook her head slowly. "I'm sorry that I've drawn you into this circus. Into the inner workings of my family."

She took a few steps to the right and then back to the left. "I'm sorry we ever lied about being in a relationship. I'm sorry I couldn't handle this party by myself."

"Em—"

She continued as if he hadn't said anything. "I'm sorry you don't want to stay here in Alexandria. I'm sorry that you don't enjoy having **your dad's bar and house, and** cute little Cosmo."

"Now, that's not entirely—"

She placed a hand on his chest to stop him and drew in a big breath. Then she looked directly into his eyes. "I'm sorry your dad wasn't there for you after your mother's death. And…I'm sorry that you truly don't see how much losing your mother has affected everything in your life."

His mother's death had happened almost two decades ago. He was over it.

Wasn't he?

He stepped back and Emerson's hand dropped.

Of course he wasn't over it. How did you ever get over the loss of a parent?

But, dammit, that wasn't controlling his life. He didn't let her death permeate other areas.

He turned on Emerson. "You don't know what you're talking about." Anger emphasized each word. How dare she say that?

Emerson didn't back down. "Actually, the problem is that I really do." She started walking away but paused and then spun back around. "Talking about your mother with me isn't what you need, Jack."

"You're an expert on what I need? Enlighten me."

"You need closure. I don't know what you need to do to get it. But I can't help you with that."

The nerve of her. Just because he had revealed a bit of his past to her the other night didn't make her some kind of expert on what he needed. "We're done here."

She nodded slowly. "I know."

"No, I mean we're done completely. This relationship is over."

She glanced down at the ground, then back up to him, and her eyes were shimmering, not just with tears, but with understanding. "I know," she repeated. "I've hurt you. It's time for you to run."

With that, she shoved past him and headed back toward the house.

I've hurt you. It's time for you to run.

What the hell did that mean? More importantly, was it true?

Jack had no idea. All he did know at the moment was that Emerson hadn't merely hurt him. She'd ripped his heart out and stomped all over it.

Without her, he had nothing left here. It truly was time to go.

Chapter Fourteen

The next morning, Jack and Xander were at The Wright Drink, bright and early, doing inventory. Correction— Jack was doing inventory. Xander was sitting around, recounting some story about a woman he'd met at the Dewitt party the night before.

Jack should be tired. He'd barely slept the night before. After making sure Grace could give Emerson a ride home, he said his goodbyes to Mr. and Mrs. Dewitt, who'd given him odd stares. Obviously, he and Emerson should have left together.

Whatever. There was no more him and Emerson.

"She was a knockout," Xander was saying. "Blond hair, big blue eyes and incredibly intelligent."

"Uh-huh."

"We were having the best conversation about Europe too, until Emerson's annoying friend stopped by."

Jack looked up. "Who, Grace?"

"Grace." Xander ground out her name between a clenched jaw. "That woman drives me nuts."

"I think she's sweet."

"What do you know?"

"A lot more than you, obviously." He'd meant it lightly, but it apparently hadn't come out that way. Xander faced him.

"Where's Cosmo?"

Customers were constantly asking about the dog. The guy who delivered the beer had questioned Jack about Cosmo's absence. Now Xander was asking about him. Apparently, his dad had often brought him into the bar. Jack had to admit it had been nice to return to his empty, lonely house, after things had ended with Emerson, to find the mutt excitedly waiting for him. As if he knew Jack had a crappy night, he'd snuggled extra-close to him in bed. Which Jack had to admit was nice. Still, he didn't belong in a bar.

"There are health codes."

Xander shrugged. "Your dad always had him in here."

Jack slammed his clipboard down just a touch too hard. "I'm not my dad."

Xander nodded slowly. "I was going to let it slide, but now my curiosity is piqued. You've been in a foul mood all morning. What gives?"

"You're supposed to be helping me with this inventory, and instead you're sitting on those boxes, waxing poetic about some blonde you met and telling me how much you hate Emerson's best friend."

Xander wagged a finger in his general direction. "Hey, did I say hate? I never said hate. *Hate* is a very strong word. Let's go with *strongly dislike*."

"Whatever," Jack muttered under his breath.

"Emerson is really cool and laid-back. Weird that she

would be friends with someone so high-strung. And annoying."

Jack really didn't want to think about Emerson right now. But unfortunately she was all he was thinking about.

He and Emerson had made an arrangement. They had lied in order to help each other. Maybe they'd taken it to the next level, but they were both healthy, consenting adults. There was nothing to feel guilty about.

So why did he feel so guilty?

He shook his head, wishing the pangs of conscience would fall right out of his head. There was no reason to feel this way. Emerson was now in a better place with her family. She just didn't see it yet.

She was on the path to standing up for herself.

Not to mention that she had a successful business and a townhouse and friends. She was fine. She *would* be fine.

He was the one who wasn't okay. He was the one hiding in a dark, dank storage room in the back of a bar.

He leaned against the shelf and closed his eyes.

"You know, hiding isn't going to help this situation," Xander said.

Jack's jaw ticked. "What situation is that?"

"The one where you messed stuff up with Emerson."

Jack opened his eyes in time to see Xander lean against the opposite shelf and cross his arms over his chest. He was dressed casually, yet still carried that aura of supreme confidence.

"You want to talk about it?"

"Not really." Jack didn't want to talk about it. None of it. And yet he found himself opening up. "We fought. Bad."

"About what?"

"I don't even know how it started." That wasn't true.

It had started because he couldn't open up to her. Because she had totally called him out on his crap. In one month, Emerson had figured him out better than pretty much anyone else in his life.

When he felt hurt, he ran.

"I was telling her about my mom—"

"Whoa. You talked about your mom with Emerson?"

"So?"

"I've known you since we were in kindergarten. You've barely talked to *me* about your mom and I was there when it…happened." Xander grabbed a bottle of water he'd brought with him and took a long swig. "She must be really special."

Jack shrugged.

"Listen, dude, you know my stance on relationships."

"Yeah, it's brilliant. Don't get into one." He turned and counted the bottles of tonic on the shelf. "Real or fake relationships. Both suck. I should have listened to you."

He heard Xander let out a long exhale. He turned to see his friend frowning. "What?"

"I'm only going to say this once and I will deny it if you ever bring it up." Xander gave a long, dramatic pause. "Sometimes I'm wrong."

Jack almost laughed. But he knew his friend was serious. "Oh yeah? And what have you been wrong about lately?"

"Relationships. Sometimes they're good. Damn good."

"You're full of crap."

"Nope. I'm not. But you are if you let Emerson get away."

"I don't want to talk about her anymore."

"You're such an idiot."

Jack shoved his shoulder as he passed him and pretended to study another shelf of inventory.

"Emerson is amazing. She's beautiful and smart and funny. You're in love with her."

Jack froze. Xander had no idea what he was talking about. He wasn't in love with Emerson or anyone else. He'd never been in love. He wouldn't let himself fall in love.

Loving a person was far too dangerous. Loving someone opened up the possibility of loss and heartache. He'd been through enough of that for a lifetime.

"Like I said, I don't want to talk about Emerson. I'm going to sell the bar."

"Jack—"

"I made up my mind. Can you call my dad's lawyer, Fred? I'd like you to be there too."

"Jack," Xander began again. "Please think about this."

He had.

Jack usually felt better after he made a decision. Right or wrong, it was empowering to simply commit to doing something.

He was going to sell The Wright Drink. It was settled.

And yet he didn't feel settled. He felt moody and indecisive. Xander had finally gotten sick of his bad mood and left the bar. Jack finished inventory, made sure his staff members were all set and took the night off.

On the drive to his dad's house, Jack found his car veering down different streets than his usual route. When he threw the car into Park outside the cemetery, he wasn't particularly surprised.

He hadn't been to visit his father's grave yet. It had been raining the day of the funeral, so instead of holding the interment graveside, they'd stayed in the mausoleum, where it had been warm and dry.

But as he walked along the winding path that would

lead him to the double plot, Jack knew that visiting his dad wasn't why he was here.

It was a nice place, as far as cemeteries went. The grass was well-kept and large oak trees lined the narrow road that wove throughout the plots and headstones.

There was a small fountain in the middle of a roundabout. The white marble attracted birds, who delighted in splashing in the water.

His mother had liked that statue. He remembered her saying so when they had visited the cemetery when he had been young. Ironically, the statue now acted as marker to her grave.

Jack turned to the right and walked a short distance, reaching the slate-gray headstone, with their names etched in the stone. When his mother had died, his father had bought his plot and the double headstone. Jack remembered thinking how morbid that was. Although, it had greatly helped him when he'd returned for his father's death.

He knelt in front of the headstone. The ground was damp. He could feel it through his jeans. But Jack didn't care.

His dad's date of death hadn't even been engraved yet. Suddenly, guilt overwhelmed him. He should have come here sooner. Or at all. In the late spring, near Memorial Day, he should plant some flowers. Geraniums. His mother always did that with her departed relatives. And she switched those flowers throughout the year. Brought wreaths at the holidays.

Of course, that would require Jack to stick around. As it were, he wouldn't be here around Memorial Day. As soon as he sold his dad's house, he wouldn't be here at all.

Sorry, Dad, he thought to himself. Jack thought his dad would understand though.

He reached a hand out and traced his father's name with his finger. Then, finally, he looked at his mother's side of the headstone. He didn't expect the quick inhale of breath or the lump that formed in his throat.

"Hi, Mom." He said it quietly, even though there was no one else in the area. He bowed his head. "I should have come sooner."

But he hadn't wanted to. Because he didn't want his mother to be here, buried in the cold, hard ground. He wanted her to be alive, bright and vibrant, with him.

Jack dropped his head into his hand. "Dammit, Mom. I miss you." Thinking of the fact that he would never see her alive again made him feel restless, annoyed, irritated.

Devastated.

The urge to take off running was overwhelming. To stand up and turn around and jog toward the front gate. To keep going through Alexandria, through Old Town, away from his father's bar and his house and everything in Virginia.

If his mother had been there, she would have given him *that* look. The mother of looks. The one that froze him in place. In fact, he felt like she was looking down on him now. He couldn't move, even though every bone in his body wanted him to.

"Well, I'm not running. Not right now. I'm here." His voice was laced with defensiveness.

"It's not like Dad and I didn't get along." He looked at his father's name again. He did love his father, and he knew his dad loved him.

"It's just that when you died, everything changed. I don't know. Maybe it would have anyway." His mother died when he was fifteen. It didn't escape Jack's notice that he'd entered adolescence.

His knees were aching from kneeling. "Hell with it."

He plopped down on the grass, feeling the dampness seep into his pants.

"It didn't feel like home without you. Nothing did," he whispered. "Not the house, not the bar, not Dad."

I was all alone.

Jack had felt so lonely and isolated during that time. That's why he ran. Ran away to college and kept going. The further he ran, the further away the pain was.

It was a heady realization, and he didn't know what to do with it. Emerson had called him out on it the night before. She had claimed he ran to escape hurt. He'd thought she was full of it. But now he had to agree.

"I'm okay though, Mom. You don't have to worry about me. You should see the bar now. It looks really good. Emerson came in and worked her magic."

He thought of Emerson and that glittery clip she'd worn in her hair. "You'd like Emerson. A lot. I do."

It struck him that Emerson and his mom had a lot in common. They both laughed at his stupid jokes. They both rolled their eyes when he was being stupid. They both loved him in spite of everything else.

Emerson brought a sparkle back into his life. A sparkle that had dimmed the day his mother had died.

Xander was right. He was in love with Emerson.

His phone let out a sound, alerting him to a text message. He pulled it out of his pocket and saw Xander's name.

Fred Koda and I will be at the bar Monday morning, at 10:00 a.m., for you to sign all of the paperwork. Less than forty-eight hours as a bar owner. Celebrate your freedom…

He frowned and stowed his phone. For someone who was about to get "freedom," Jack certainly didn't feel light and easygoing. In fact, he felt rather encumbered and stressed.

Jack vividly remembered that summer after high school graduation. He'd left for college early to report for training. As he'd driven away from Alexandria, he'd felt like a million bucks. The world had been at his feet and he had finally been able to breathe.

He had felt about the exact opposite of how he was feeling at the moment.

When he'd left at eighteen, he hadn't felt like he was leaving home. Instead he felt like he was finally out, searching for it. But somehow that journey brought him back to where it had all started. And the place that had made him feel so alone suddenly was the only place where he wanted to stay.

Because this is where Emerson was.

Emerson challenged him. She constantly surprised him. And she'd reminded him that he wasn't in this world alone.

She was home for him now.

Jack didn't quite know what to do with this newfound revelation. He was selling the bar in two days and putting his dad's house up for sale. What about Emerson?

She had fallen out of a window and had landed in his heart.

Chapter Fifteen

Emerson felt like crap.

She spent most of the weekend snuggled up in her bed, watching mindless TV shows and eating food with way too many calories. It was easy to get lost in the problems of the Real Housewives while shoving cold pizza in her mouth. That way she didn't have to think about what was actually bothering her.

Jack Wright.

Falling out of that window had turned out to be the best thing she'd ever done. Even if Jack really left town, her life was better for having him in it for that short time. She felt stronger around him. More confident. She felt like herself.

Still, these recent revelations didn't keep the heartache at bay. And she was suffering.

Usually Mondays were a light workday for her. She caught up on paperwork and reviewed files for her coming events. She'd been looking forward to the mindless work. It would require her attention just enough to keep it from drifting back to Jack.

But her mother had called early that morning and asked—more like demanded—her presence at Dewitt's Bridal. Something about new dresses and inventory and help with the computer system. Whatever. The last place Emerson wanted to go was her mother's bridal shop.

Try saying no to Beatrice Dewitt. A near-to-impossible task.

She and Jack had left her parents' party separately, something that had definitely drawn the attention of her parents. For once in her life, though, they hadn't badgered her with questions. Something told her she wouldn't be so lucky this morning. No way could she escape the questions when she was alone with her mother.

So at exactly nine thirty in the morning, she made her way into the shop begrudgingly. The weather mirrored her mood. It was gray and overcast, with a harsh wind whipping the curls around her face.

Since the shop was closed at the moment, she dug through her purse for her set of spare keys. The bells situated over the door signaled her arrival. Her mother immediately came out of her office.

"Emerson, there you are."

"It's nine thirty. I'm not late," she said, with irritation coating each word. "You said to get here at nine thirty."

It was a rare outburst for her, and her mother responded to it with narrowed eyes. Strangely, she didn't comment or reprimand her.

"Well, come in then. Do you want anything to drink? Coffee? Tea?"

"I'm not one of your brides, Mama. I know where all

of the drinks are kept. If I want something, I'll go get it for myself."

Beatrice arched one perfectly plucked brow but still remained silent.

Emerson shimmied out of her coat and threw it onto a chair. "I'm here. What do you need? I do have a job of my own. Besides, I don't understand why your actual employee isn't here. You know, my sister."

"That's three sassy comments in a row. You've reached your limit."

No matter how infuriating her mother could be, no matter how much she drove Emerson nuts, she was still her mother. And deep down, she didn't like to disappoint her. To make her angry or upset.

But glancing at her now, Emerson didn't see anger or hurt on her face. Instead it was pure concern. And that was her undoing.

She sunk down to the chair she'd just thrown her coat. Tears threatened but Emerson took a deep breath to hold them in. Next thing she knew, a finger was under her chin, forcing her head up.

"What is it, Emerson?"

As if she was still ten years old, she launched herself into her mother's arms. When was the last time she'd done that?

"Oh Mama, it's over between me and Jack," she muttered against her mother's gorgeous blue cashmere sweater. She leaned back. "I'm sorry I'm crying all over your sweater."

"That doesn't matter."

"It does. I've messed everything up. Just like I always do."

"Oh honey, what are you talking about?"

"How I've always screwed up. My whole life. No wonder you're always disappointed in me."

Her mother shook her gently. "Disappointed? Emerson Rose, this is ridiculous. Stop it right now."

"But I never did anything right. Not in elementary school. Or what about how I wasn't homecoming queen or a cheerleader? I didn't go to the college you wanted me to go to. And—and I didn't get married."

Beatrice's face paled. "Emerson, have you been under the impression that you've disappointed me somehow?"

"Of course."

Her mother opened and closed her mouth. Not that she would ever point it out, Emerson saw a line form in the middle of her mother's forehead. She knew that line. Her mother was thinking. After a few silent moments, Beatrice nodded firmly.

"It has been said that I am not the warmest of women."

It was Emerson's turn to drop her mouth open.

Beatrice smiled. "But I can admit when I'm wrong. I probably have given you the impression I'm unhappy with you."

Emerson shuffled her feet and glanced down at the recently vacuumed rug. "You've kinda given me that impression most of my life."

Beatrice sighed and closed her eyes. When she opened them, her gaze was determined. "I'm your mother. It is my job to be hard on you." She reached forward and tucked a curl behind Emerson's ear. "Perhaps I've done my job a little too well. Maybe I should have eased up on you a tad."

"Uh—uh…," Emerson stuttered and then finally dropped back into the chair.

"You are a forward-thinking, independent woman, Emerson. You always have been. I never worried about your activities or college. In fact, your father and I were ecstatic that you got accepted into such a good university. And you did all of the applications and admission work yourself. Then you started your own business. You didn't even ask either of us for help. Even though we would have loved nothing more."

"Really?"

"Of course. My goodness, Emerson. You've accomplished so much in your life."

"Professionally. But not personally."

Beatrice tapped a finger to her lip as she considered her. "What does that mean?"

"I'm not married like Amelia is. I mean I was almost... I mean I know that it was embarrassing when Thad left me at the altar."

"Naturally." Beatrice froze. "Wait a minute. Are you saying it was embarrassing for me? For your father?"

Emerson nodded and felt a lump forming in her throat.

"Oh sweetheart, the only embarrassing thing about that situation is that I didn't go find that little weasel and punch him in the face."

"Mama!"

"Well, it's true. He was a scoundrel for what he did to you. A coward and a liar and a real piece of sh—"

"Mama. Ohmigod." The giggle that burst from her lips actually felt good. But only for a moment. "Still, what happened with me and Thad was bad."

"You were engaged, Emerson. It didn't work out. That's not the end of the world. He did you a favor. You don't want to be married to someone like that."

Beatrice crouched down in front of her. She reached for her hands and Emerson willingly linked fingers with her mom.

"Is there anything else bothering you?"

Emerson couldn't believe how much she'd said to her mother already. Even more surprising was how well her mother was taking everything. At this point, she might as well keep going.

Isn't that what Jack would tell her? To stick up for herself?

"My whole life I've felt like I'm not good enough. I never measured up to Amelia. She was the golden child and I was a big screwup."

Pain, pure and simple, flashed on Beatrice's face. "You don't have to compete with your sister. Not ever." She squeezed Emerson's hands tightly. "Why would you want to, honestly?"

"Excuse me?"

"Amelia's not happy. I wouldn't be either if Charlie were my husband."

She felt like she'd just fallen down the rabbit hole. What the what? "Mama! I can't believe you just said that."

"She's right though."

Emerson and her mother both turned in shock to find Amelia standing there. She'd come in through the back door. They both jumped up.

"Mia," Emerson said on an exhale. "Ohmigod. I'm so sorry you heard that."

"Sweetheart," Beatrice began walking toward her daughter.

Amelia held her hand up to stop both of them. "Don't be sorry. Charlie is a horrible husband. To be honest, he's not even that great a person."

There must be something in the air today. Emerson chewed on a nail as she studied her sister, waiting for her to say she was kidding. But that didn't happen. Amelia's face was calm and her demeanor steady.

"Did something happen between you and Charlie?" she asked.

"Nothing happened. That's kind of the point. Charlie is absent. He's disinterested. He's boring. I follow him around when he travels for work, but he never makes time for me. I know he likes showing me off to his friends and colleagues. I feel like a glorified lawn ornament."

"An absolutely gorgeous lawn ornament," Emerson said loyally.

Mia chuckled, then grew serious again. "I feel like I don't have any interests of my own. I don't really have a life to be proud of." A tear escaped her eye. "I don't have a life at all. Not like you." She looked at Emerson.

Emerson's heart broke for her little sister.

"Don't pity me, Em. It's my own fault." She swiped at the solitary tear. "I just kinda always went with the flow. I never attempted to branch out and do anything on my own. But you know what? I'm done."

"What does that mean exactly?" Beatrice asked.

"I know I want more out of life. I'm not sure where to start, so the first thing I'm going to do is file for divorce. My marriage is over."

Emerson watched her sister, expecting tears and shaking. Instead of seeing sadness though, what she noticed was an overwhelming sense of relief.

Beatrice crossed to Amelia. She paused and then grabbed her daughter in a fierce hug. "About time."

They broke apart and Amelia actually laughed. "About time? We've only been married six months."

"Six months too long, if you ask me. What do you think, Emerson?"

"Totally."

"If you both felt this way, why did you never say anything?"

Beatrice sighed. "Because you were so intent on marrying him. I know how stubborn you can be when your mind is set on something."

Well, how about that, Emerson thought. She definitely didn't give her mother enough credit. Apparently she was attuned to everything going on with her daughters.

"You know what we need right now?" Beatrice said, clapping her hands together. She didn't answer right away. Instead she ran to her office and returned with a bottle of bourbon. "Something to take the edge off."

"Mama," Emerson said as Amelia's mouth dropped open. "You keep a bottle of bourbon in your office?"

"Scotch, wine and a little gin too." She winked. "How do you think I get through dealing with some of those tough bridezillas?"

Emerson's whole world was turning upside down. To be honest, she kind of liked the view from this side.

"Who wants some?" Beatrice waved the bottle.

"We need glasses," Amelia said.

"Says who? The bourbon police?"

Yep, the world was on its head.

"What happened to our prim and proper mama?" Amelia asked, tentatively accepting the bottle.

"Girls, the world is not black-and-white. There are all types of gray. You can be polite and have good manners without being a stodgy, boring dud. Speaking of gray..." She tapped her finger against her mouth.

"What?" Emerson tilted her head. She followed her mother's gaze to the other side of the store. Her eyes raked over the mounds of dresses, but she didn't see anything out of order.

Beatrice pointed at Amelia. "The silver dress. It just came in a couple of weeks ago. You know the one?"

"Very 1920s-inspired. With the beading?"

"That's the one."

She rushed off to the other side of the store and returned carrying a gorgeous sleeveless silver gown. It was covered in beading, had a V-shaped neckline and hung straight down to the ground. It was a modern version of a gown that could have been in *The Great Gatsby*.

"That's gorgeous," Emerson said, unable to hold in the wistful sigh.

And it was. Different. Unique. Unlike so many of the cookie-cutter gowns that cluttered the store.

"I think this would look exquisite on you."

Amelia began clapping her hands together. "Yes. You have to try this on, Em." Amelia came to her and squeezed her hands.

Emerson broke away and backed up. "No, no, no." She threw her hands up in front of her.

"Yes, yes, yes." Beatrice also stepped forward. "Time to fully let go of your past and all of your hang-ups about weddings and wedding dresses."

"Mama," she groaned. "I can't."

Beatrice stepped forward and framed her face with her hands. "Yes, you can. You are my strong Emerson."

She didn't know how it happened, but ten minutes later she was standing in front of the three-way mirrors, wearing the gorgeous silver dress, which fit her to a tee. Except for the length, it almost didn't even need an alteration.

"This is amazing," she whispered reverently.

"It really, truly is," Amelia agreed.

Emerson turned to her mother and almost fell off the pedestal. Beatrice Dewitt had tears in her eyes.

She exhaled. "That's simply perfect." She coughed and dabbed at her eyes. "You need a headpiece. I'll be back."

Emerson exchanged a glance with her sister. "Wow. Didn't see that coming."

"I did. You look amazing. This is the dress you need to wear when you get married."

Emerson sighed. "If that even happens."

"Of course it's going to happen. You're young and beautiful. Plus you have that hottie boyfriend."

"Yeah, well, I may have messed that up royally."

Amelia shook her head back and forth. "I don't know. Have you seen the way that man looks at you?"

"You've mentioned that."

"Thad never even compared to him, you know."

Emerson went sentimental. "I'm over Thad. I really am. In fact, I don't think I loved him at all."

"You think?"

"I know."

"How do you know?" Amelia asked.

"Because I didn't get *that* feeling with Thad. You know, that kind of tingly feeling. The one that makes your head all fuzzy and your knees weak."

"I've never experienced anything close to that kind of feeling with Charlie. Or with any of my boyfriends, really."

"I have. With Jack," she whispered.

Beatrice came back in, carrying two different veils. She took a turn holding each up to Emerson. Then shook her head. "Nope, neither of these work with the dress."

"I don't think she should wear a veil at all. Maybe just something sparkly, like a headband or something," Amelia offered.

Emerson started playing with her hair, pulling the curls up into a loose ponytail. "Maybe something like this. Then some kind of headband or clip here." Her mother grinned. "What?"

"See, wedding dresses aren't so bad."

Emerson let her hair fall back down. She ran a hand down the column of the dress. It really was stunning. And she truly loved how it looked on her.

She could see herself standing at an altar. Not in a church, but maybe at a vineyard. Something that had a nice room that opened onto a patio. Under some kind of gazebo. With twinkly lights strung from wall to wall.

Her sister would be there, and her parents, of course. But the crowd wouldn't be too large. Just immediate family and close friends. Grace and Amelia would be her bridesmaids.

A white cake would sit off in one corner of the room. Cascading flowers decked out in glitter to match her dress would tumble down one side of it.

She closed her eyes. She could almost smell the flowers, taste the wine on her tongue, hear the sounds of the string quartet. Her eyes opened and she took another peek at herself in the mirror.

The dress was perfect. The vision was perfect.

Jack was perfect.

She shook her head. Jack wasn't perfect. He was just perfect for her.

And he was leaving. Her eyes widened and she hiccupped to hold in a tear.

Her mother stepped up onto the pedestal. "What is it, Emerson?"

"Jack's leaving me." Her voice wavered as she said those three horrible words out loud.

"Oh Em." Amelia joined them, as well.

"I don't want him to go."

Beatrice pushed a curl behind her ear. "What do you want?"

"I want him to stay. I want him to keep the bar, because I think it means more to him than he'll admit. I want him to realize how much he needs Cosmo in his life, because he's such a good doggy dad. And I want... I want him to be with me."

"Does he know that?" Amelia asked.

Sadly, she shook her head

"I didn't say anything when you were dating Thad," Her mother said. She looked at Amelia. "And I haven't said anything about you and Charlie. Well, that stops now. I'm butting in." She took Emerson by the shoulders. "Don't let Jack get away."

"But our whole relationship has been a lie. We started out playing pretend." Her hand flew to her mouth as soon as the words were out.

Her mother and sister stared at her. So she told them everything. When she was done, she waited for the disappointment. What she didn't expect was for her mother to seem skeptical.

"I absolutely don't like that you and Jack lied to all of us. And climbing out of that window in the Pnina dress— I could just strangle you. However, we've all seen you together. You may have started out playing pretend, but trust me, the two of you evolved into a very real couple. There's just one question left."

She tilted her head. "What's that?"

"What are you going to do about it?"

Her mother stepped back and yanked on Amelia's hand to bring her with her. That left Emerson alone on the pedestal.

"You want Jack Wright? Go get him."

"I...uh, I..." Emerson bit her lip. She took another look at her reflection. She made a beautiful bride. Jack had told her that when this had all begun. He was right. The only thing missing was her groom.

A smile blossomed on her face. She turned to her mother and sister and offered a strong nod. "You're right. You're so freaking right. I love Jack. And it's about time he knows it."

She jumped down and frantically searched for her shoes. She slipped her feet into the loafers and wondered where her coat was. Realizing she was wasting time, she gave up the search and started for the door.

"Em, what are you doing? Where are you going?"

"To see Jack."

As suddenly as the urge to run to her pretend boy-friend filled her, the excitement dissipated. Emerson froze and then slowly turned back to her mother and sister. She shook her head.

"No. Nope. I'm not going to run to him."

"And why is that?" Beatrice asked, with a knowing twinkle in her eye.

"Because if Jack really wants to be with me, then he needs to realize that. He needs to come to me. I'm good enough just the way I am."

Her mother enfolded her into a fierce hug. "About time you realize what the rest of us already see."

Emerson smiled on the outside. She felt lighter and more confident. But as she walked to the window at the back of the dressing room—the window she'd climbed out of not that long ago—she was still hurting on the inside. She wanted Jack.

But there was now something she wanted just as much. Happiness for herself.

Chapter Sixteen

"You're sure about this?"

Jack nodded at Fred Koda's question. He didn't even need to take the time to think on his decision. It may not please everyone, but in his heart, he knew it was right.

Time to take a new step in life.

"Given everything that's happened over the last couple of weeks, I want to make sure you're thinking clearly. Are you positive you know what you're doing here?"

Jack offered his oldest friend a wry grin. Then he clasped Xander on the back. "I thought you would agree with my decision." He knew where Xander stood on the matter.

As if offering his support, Cosmo let out a little yip. Jack leaned down and rubbed a hand over the dog's head.

"I think Cosmo agrees with me," Jack said.

"And I thought you were so strict about not bringing him into the bar," Xander said, with one eyebrow arching in question.

"Well, it's a big day. I thought my new roommate would want in on it."

Jack rolled Xander's fancy pen over and over in his hands. Why anyone thought to spend such an absurd amount of money on a writing utensil was beyond him. He handed it back over to Xander.

Fred shuffled through the papers on the table where the three of them were sitting. "Looks like all the right lines have been signed." He reached over and clasped Jack's hand firmly. Silently, they shook hands.

Xander said, "I think we're all done here."

The three of them stood. Anticipating activity, Cosmo popped up as well, with his tail wagging.

Jack grinned. "Well...not quite." He turned to Xander. "Do me a favor and man the bar?"

Xander straightened the tie that complemented what had to be a very expensive business suit. "For how long? I'm not exactly dressed for the occasion."

"I'm not sure. If I'm back in a couple of minutes, you'll know it didn't go well."

"Fine. Can Mr. Cosmo stay with me?"

"No way. I need him for moral support. Plus who can say no to his face?"

He didn't give Xander another chance to speak, because he was already leashing Cosmo up and heading toward the door. Sensing something exciting was happening, Cosmo was extra animated.

It would have taken Jack a minute to walk around the block, but the dog had other ideas. "Must you pee on every blade of grass?" he asked Cosmo. The dog just lifted his leg one more time.

Finally, he reached the bridal boutique. "This is it, Cosmo. Wish me luck." Taking a huge breath, he pulled the door open and stepped inside to a land of white puffiness and sparkles and all things bridal.

He walked through the store for a few minutes before he heard voices coming from the dressing rooms. Jack picked up Cosmo and headed in that direction.

He rapped his knuckles on the open door before stepping inside. Mrs. Dewitt and Amelia both turned in his direction. Shock initially registered on their faces. But then Amelia grinned and Mrs. Dewitt narrowed her eyes.

He gulped. But then he looked to the right and saw her. Emerson was at the window, peering out.

She was an absolute vision. Her auburn hair a curly mess around her face. And she was wearing the most beautiful silver dress. Jack had never seen anything so beautiful in his entire life.

"Emerson," he said.

She whipped around and stumbled. He darted across the room and grabbed her arm to steady her. But then she stepped back.

"Climbing out another window?" he asked, going for light and humorous. But feeling the room, he quickly realized it wasn't the time for that. "I have some things to say."

He turned and handed Cosmo to Mrs. Dewitt.

"If this dog pees or chews on one single thing in this store, I will skin you alive," she said to Jack. Then she looked down at Cosmo, who stuck his little tongue out and licked her chin. Her face softened. "Aren't you such a cutie? How sweet."

"He won't damage anything," Jack tried to assure her.

"The same cannot be said for me." She kissed Cosmo on the head and then stared Jack down with such intensity that he started considering climbing out the window himself.

"I do not appreciate being lied to. While I understand you were helping my daughter—"

"Mama," Amelia interrupted. "I want to hear what he has to say. Let's hold off on grilling him for a second."

"Thanks, Amelia," Jack said gratefully. "Would you two mind if we had a little privacy?"

Neither of them moved.

"I would like to talk to Emerson in private," he tried again.

"No," Mrs. Dewitt said.

He could argue, but Jack had a feeling he wouldn't come close to winning. Instead he turned back to Emerson, who hadn't uttered a peep since he'd barged in.

"Em, I just met with Xander and Fred Koda, my dad's lawyer."

Emerson's face fell and it seemed like her entire body deflated. "Oh. You did it then?"

"Yeah," he said. His voice was husky and there was nothing he could do to stop it. Just seeing her standing there in that dress was forcing his heart to beat in a staccato rhythm. It was hard to keep up with it.

"You're really leaving then?"

What? He closed his eyes. He was doing this all wrong.

Jack crossed back to Emerson and took her hands in his. "I didn't sell the bar."

Amelia gasped behind him, but Emerson remained still. She wasn't going to make this easy on him. But he deserved that.

"I didn't sell," he tried again. "In fact, I made a decision. I'm going to stay here with Cosmo and run it myself. My dad's bar. Well, now it's my bar."

"What made you change your mind?" she asked cautiously.

After Jack had visited his mom in the cemetery, he'd

returned home to another sleepless night. He realized he was in love with Emerson. He knew he wanted to spend his life with her.

Still, comprehending these new feelings hadn't come easily. Years of running away threatened to overtake him.

But he'd spent all day Sunday trying to imagine what his life without Emerson would be like. Maybe he would meet someone new. But he knew that wouldn't do. There would never be anyone else like her.

She was his everything.

"You did. You made me change my mind, Emerson."

"And why is that?" Mrs. Dewitt asked from behind him. He turned and winked at her.

"Because I'm in love with you, Emerson Rose Dewitt. I know we haven't known each other that long and we've been lying to everyone for most of that time."

"Which is wrong and we will be discussing later," Mrs. Dewitt added.

"Mama, shush," Amelia said.

"I'm so crazy in love with you. I can't imagine my life without you in it. Before I met you, everything was dull and dark. But then you climbed out of a window and all of a sudden, the lights turned on. You bring a sparkle to my life that I haven't felt since my mother was alive."

As he watched her eyes widen and her mouth fall open, he couldn't think of any other words to say. Instead he pulled her to him and crushed his mouth to hers.

The kiss was a total-mind-and-body experience. He poured everything into it. Every feeling, fear and desire. Emerson met him at every turn.

When they parted, her eyes slowly opened and met his.

"I love you too," she whispered.

"You do?"

She nodded. "Oh yeah."

"Good, because…well…" He looked back at Mrs. De-witt, who, if he wasn't mistaken, was wiping a tear from her eyes. "I'm not exactly doing this right."

She waved a hand at him. "No, no, it's perfect. Keep going."

He chuckled and turned back to the love of his life. Jack squeezed her hands and then got down on one knee.

"Ohmigod," Amelia screeched.

"Emerson," he began. "I have nothing to offer you."

She bent over and kissed him. "You have everything because you're my everything."

"Please marry me."

It was probably only a second, but to Jack, it felt like a lifetime. A huge smile broke out on her face before she said, "Yes, yes, of course I'll marry you."

He flew up and kissed her again. Cosmo ran over and started jumping around them. They broke apart and laughed.

He knew with every ounce of his being that she was the most right decision he'd ever made in his life. Everything—all the running and all the hiding—was worth it because it eventually brought him to her.

Jack kissed the tip of her nose. "You make the most beautiful bride."

"I seem to have heard that before."

He reached down and scooped up Cosmo. One arm around Emerson and one holding his dog. A perfect little family. "Do you believe me this time?"

She nodded.

"Do you also believe that I love you and that I want to spend the rest of my life with you?"

"Depends," she said, brushing a hand over his cheek. "Do you believe that I love you too and that I can't wait to start spending the rest of my life with you?"

Together, completely in sync, they said, "I do."

Amelia gasped. "Wait, this isn't right! The groom isn't supposed to see the bride in her dress before the wedding. It's bad luck."

Beatrice smiled. "I think, in this case, it won't matter at all."

"Cheers to Emerson and Jack!"

"Thanks, Mia." Emerson touched her champagne flute to her sister's, then repeated the gesture with her parents and Xander. Finally, she turned to Jack. Their eyes met and held.

"To the future Mrs. Wright," Jack said quietly, as he wrapped an arm around her.

"To our future," she said and kissed him.

She couldn't believe it. She was engaged. To her once-fake boyfriend—the man she truly loved. But more than that, she was so happy that Jack was putting down roots in his hometown. He was keeping his dad's bar. He told her about visiting his parents' graves, and somehow, he seemed more at ease than she'd ever seen him before. He'd made peace.

Cosmo jumped up on her leg, making his presence known. "And cheers to you too," she said, reaching down to scratch behind his ears. His tail wagged excitedly and his little pink tongue lolled out of the side of his mouth.

They were gathered in the alley behind The Wright Drink. She and Jack thought it was the appropriate place to celebrate their engagement. Of course, they had to relay the story of how they met again.

They'd waited until the evening, so her dad could join them after work. When Walter arrived, Jack had pulled him aside, apologizing for not asking for his blessing before proposing. Her dad was all smiles though.

"I asked Beatrice to marry me in a similar way. I just blurted it out."

"And here we are thirty years later," Beatrice added.

Emerson let out a huge sigh of relief. For the first time in her entire life, everything felt absolutely right. She'd dared to wish for more than what she had, and shockingly, she got it all.

"Should we go inside for more champagne?" Amelia asked.

"Yes, though it has been charming standing out in this dirty alley with the enticing aroma of trash," Beatrice said, with one perfectly raised eyebrow.

Emerson laughed. Her mother had not been too keen on coming out here in the first place. But after their talk this morning, she knew that her mother supported her. And loved her. And thought she was fine just as she was.

It was more than she could have ever wanted.

She reached for her mother's hand and led the way back inside The Wright Drink, where the music was going on the jukebox, the TVs above the bar were set to a variety of sports and news channels and the drinks and food were flowing. It looked inviting and fun. Just as she'd envisioned.

The family and Xander congregated on one side of the bar. Oscar broke out another bottle of champagne and Jack announced that everyone in the bar was getting a drink on him.

The chimes above the front door sounded and Emerson turned to see her best friend enter.

"Emerson," Grace screamed. "O-M-G! You're engaged." She raced down the steps, dashed through the room, and practically ran Emerson over in her excitement. Grace hugged her so tightly Emerson thought a rib or two may have cracked.

Happy tears pooled in Grace's eyes. "I am so freaking happy for you."

"I couldn't tell at all," Jack said with a big grin.

"Shut up," Grace said and launched herself at him for another big hug. "Congratulations. You're getting the best woman on the planet."

"I agree," Jack said.

As Grace continued her animated delight, Xander returned from the restroom. Grace's enthusiasm died and her smile faded.

"Xander," she said dryly.

"Grace," he replied with the same amount of irritation.

"Isn't it nice when two people get engaged? Don't you just love celebrating love?" she asked him.

Xander rolled his eyes. "It's what I live for."

Jack snorted. "Okay, you two. No sniping today. Only celebrating."

Grace turned from Xander and her smile returned. "In that case, I'll need a glass of that champagne."

As Oscar passed another flute across the bar, the front door opened again and a huge group of girls—at least a dozen—waltzed in the front door. They were talking excitedly amongst themselves until they stopped and looked around the bar. Emerson held her breath. She hoped they were impressed with what they saw.

"This place is so cute," one of them said.

"Has it always been here?" another asked.

She gave Jack a little nudge. "Go," she whispered.

While Jack welcomed the group and got them set up at a long table, Emerson took a moment to glance around the bar. For a Monday, there was actually quite a crowd. Besides the table of women and her family, most of the seats around the bar were occupied. She'd helped Jack work on happy hour specials, and she was happy to see people taking advantage.

Cosmo was happily prancing around the bar, going from table to table to greet the patrons. Everyone seemed delighted to meet him. He received more belly rubs and scratches than ever.

"You did this." Jack had come up behind her and wrapped his arms around her waist.

She turned in his arms, so she could look into his eyes. "We did this."

"Together," he said. He nipped her earlobe. "I have something for you. Come here a moment." He led her back through the bar and out into the alley once again.

"What are we doing out here?" she asked.

Jack pulled a small box from his pocket. "I thought I should give you this in the same spot where we met."

He opened the lid, and she gasped. "Ohmigod, Jack, that is stunning."

The ring was gorgeous. It was an antique platinum ring with a vibrant ruby in the center, surrounded by tiny diamonds.

"It was my mother's," Jack said, his gruff voice revealing deep emotions. "If you don't like it, or you want to add something to it, we can do that."

"Are you kidding? I couldn't love anything more. I'm honored to wear your mother's ring."

"She would have loved you." He slipped the ring on her finger.

"It's a perfect fit," she said, wiggling her fingers so she could watch the ring sparkle.

"So are we," Jack said. Then he reached down, put one arm under her legs and other behind her back, and lifted her into his arms. "This is more how we met."

She laughed. "Without the cumbersome wedding gown."

"But you were such a beautiful bride."

She tilted her head and met his lips for a long, sultry kiss. "And I will be again."

"But this time you'll be my bride," Jack said, his eyes darkening.

"And you'll be my groom."

The sun began to set as they kissed again, sealing their arrangement—for real this time.

* * * * *

*Look for Grace and Xavier's story,
the next book in author Kerri Carpenter's
Something True miniseries
for Harlequin Special Edition
Coming soon!*

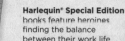

"The two of you are still married," Liz said.

"Still?" Lulu croaked.

Sam asked, "What are you talking about?"

"More to the point, how do you know this?" Lulu
demanded, the news continuing to hit her like a gut punch.

Travis looked down at the papers in front of him.
"Official state records show you eloped in the Double
Knot Wedding Chapel in Memphis, Tennessee, on
Monday, March 14, nearly ten years ago. Alongside
another couple, Peter and Theresa Thompson, in a double
wedding ceremony."

Lulu gulped. "But our union was never legal," she
pointed out, trying to stay calm, while Sam sat beside her
in stoic silence.

Liz countered, "Ah, actually, it is legal. In fact, it's still
valid to this day."

Sam reached over and took her hand in his, much as he had the first time they had been in this room together.

"How is that possible?" Lulu asked weakly.

"We never mailed in the certificate of marriage, along with the license, to the state of Tennessee," Sam said.

"And for our union to be recorded and therefore legal, we had to have done that," Lulu reiterated.

"Well, apparently, the owners of the Double Knot Wedding Chapel did, and your marriage was recorded. And is still valid to this day, near as we can tell. Unless you two got a divorce or an annulment somewhere else? Say another country?" Travis prodded.

"Why would we do that? We didn't know we were married," Sam returned.

Don't miss
Their Inherited Triplets *by Cathy Gillen Thacker,*
available August 2019 wherever
Harlequin® Special Edition books and ebooks are sold.

www.Harlequin.com

SPECIAL EXCERPT FROM

HQN™

Read on for a sneak peek at
the first funny and heart-tugging book in Jo McNally's
Rendezvous Falls series, Slow Dancing at Sunrise!

"I'd have thought the idea of me getting caught in a rainstorm would make your day."

He gave her a quick glance. Just because she was off-limits didn't mean he was blind.

"Trust me, it did." Luke slowed the truck and reached behind the seat to grab his zippered hoodie hanging there. Whitney looked down and her cheeks flamed when she realized how her clothes were clinging to her. She snatched the hoodie from his hand before he could give it to her, and thrust her arms into it without offering any thanks. Even the zipper sounded pissed off when she yanked it closed.

"Perfect. Another guy with more testosterone than manners. Nice to know it's not just a Chicago thing. Jackasses are everywhere."

Luke frowned. He'd been having fun at her expense, figuring she'd give it right back to him as she had before. But her words hinted at a story that didn't reflect well on men in general. She'd been hurt. He shouldn't care. But that quick dimming of the fight in her eyes made him feel ashamed. *That* was a new experience.

A flash of lightning made her flinch. But the thunder didn't follow as quickly as the last time. The storm was moving off. He drove from the vineyard into the parking lot and over to the main house. The sound of the rain on the roof was less angry. But Whitney wasn't. She was clutching his sweatshirt around herself, her knuckles white. From anger? Embarrassment? Both? Luke shook his head.

"Look, I thought I was doing the right thing, driving up there." He rubbed the back of his neck and grimaced, remembering how sweaty and filthy he still was. "It's not my fault you walked out of the woods soaking wet. I mean, I try not to be a jackass, but I'm still a man. And I *did* offer my hoodie."

Whitney's chin pointed up toward the second floor of the main house. Her neck was long and graceful. There was a vein pulsing at the base of it. She blinked a few times, and for a horrifying moment, he thought there might be tears shimmering there in her eyes. *Damn it.* The last thing he needed was to have Helen's niece *crying* in his truck. He opened his mouth to say something—anything—but she beat him to it.

"I'll concede I wasn't prepared for rain." Her mouth barely moved, her words forced through clenched teeth. "But a gentleman would have looked away or…something."

His low laughter was enough to crack that brittle shell of hers. She turned to face him, eyes wide.

"See, Whitney, that's where you made your biggest mistake." He shrugged. "It wasn't going out for a day hike with a storm coming." He talked over her attempted objection. "Your *biggest* mistake was thinking I'm any kind of gentleman."

The corner of her mouth tipped up into an almost smile. "But you said you weren't a jackass."

"There's a hell of a lot of real estate between jackass and gentleman, babe."

Her half smile faltered, then returned. That familiar spark appeared in her eyes. The crack in her veneer had been repaired, and the sharp edge returned to her voice. Any other guy might have been annoyed, but Luke was oddly relieved to see Whitney back in fighting form.

"The fact that you just referred to me as 'babe' tells me you're a lot closer to jackass than you think."

He lifted his shoulder. "I never told you which end of the spectrum I fell on."

The rain had slowed to a steady drizzle. She reached for the door handle, looking over her shoulder with a smirk.

"Actually, I'm pretty sure you just did."

She hurried up the steps to the covered porch. He waited, but she didn't look back before going into the house. Her energy still filled the cab of the truck, and so did her scent. Spicy, woodsy, rain soaked. Finally coming to his senses, he threw the truck into Reverse and headed back toward the carriage house. He needed a long shower. A long *cold* one.

Don't miss
Jo McNally's Slow Dancing at Sunrise,
available July 2019 from HQN Books!

www.Harlequin.com